LOST IN PROVIDENCE

TO AL AND
CATHARINA —
THANKS FOR BUYING
MY BOOK! ENJOY!
♡ JOYCE RASKIN
12/27/15

BACK TO
CONNECTICUT

EAT ME
I ♥ NY
DOWN THE RABB
HOLE
TRA

LOST IN PROVIDENCE

Short Tales of Artists in Transit

LOST IN PROVIDENCE

Short Tales of Artists in Transit

Written and Illustrated by

Joyce Raskin

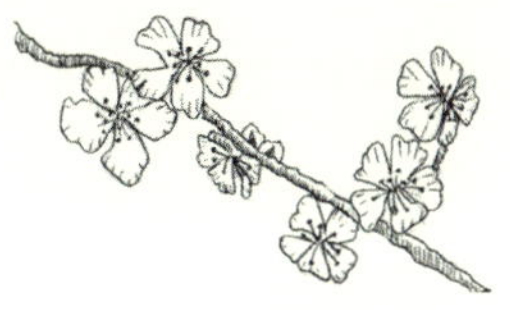

Story and plot in collaboration
with **Bre Goldsmith**

Edited by **Guy Benoit**
and **Joyce Raskin**

Number One Fan Press 2015

Dedicated to artists of all kinds, lovers of art

and anyone with an artistic sensibility

NEVER STOP CREATING

Number One Fan Press © 2015

ISBN-13: 978-0-9965116-1-2

Text is 12pt Garamond

For more information please contact: joyce.raskin@gmail.com

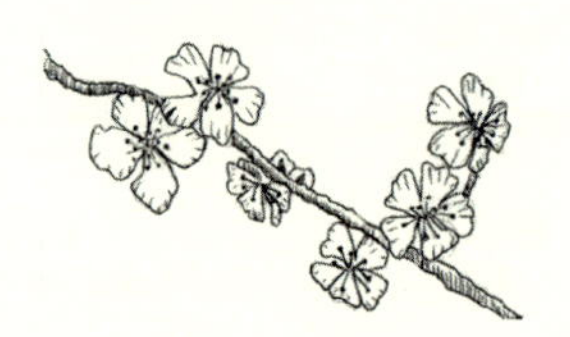

Portrait of The Artist as a Young Man

Nick Shelby was born into this world a small, weak, bit of a thing struggling to survive. The little baby boy named Nicholas Thomas Shelby limply nursed at his mother's breast and had to be fed rice milk in a bottle to keep from losing weight at a rapid pace. There were many trips to the hospital, fevers, croup, bronchitis, and pneumonia. It was a full sleepless year for Nicholas and his two young parents. Within two years Nicholas eventually grew into a healthy (but underweight) toddler ready to explore the world. Nicholas wasn't a wanderer but instead preferred stationary activities such as playing with pots of water in the kitchen, looking at colorful picture books, and drawing with crayons on paper. While a peaceful existence encircled the toddler in one room of the small apartment he called home (the kitchen), in the next room over, a small war was beginning. It was a war fueled by resentment and alcohol. For another year, Nicholas remained outside the battlefield. It was a war of words, and while Nicholas was beginning to understand some of the words, he knew nothing else.

At three years of age, a mere black ballpoint pen sent Nicholas straight to the front lines—without any armor, without any weapon, and completely unaware. The black ballpoint pen was lying innocuously on the wooden kitchen table. Nicholas had seen his mother use this very pen to write on papers. Nicholas picked up the pen and drew some marks on a few pieces of his drawing paper at the wooden table in the kitchen. What goes on in the brain of a three-year old? Well, most of us can't remember or will ever know. On this day, his brain directed Nicholas to see the empty wooden table as a canvas to make his mark with the new tool he had discovered. After exactly one hour, on this same day, every inch of the table had completely covered with the pen marks of three-year old Nicholas. He sat back in his the chair and smiled. It was at this exact moment of artistic reflection that the first shot was fired in his direction, and the front lines appeared before him. Nicholas's father appeared in the doorway. Nicholas smiled at him and pointed, "Look Daddy! Look what I did!"

His father's face at this point quickly changed in an instant as his gigantic figure simultaneously moved quickly towards Nicholas. He picked Nicholas up and threw him down on the floor and screamed, "What is wrong with *you!*" Nicholas stayed still. His mother appeared and she screamed at her husband, "What have *you* done!" His mother slowly walked over to Nicholas and picked up the boy in her arms and screamed, "Get out of this house! *Now!*" Nicholas's father bellowed and pointed with his fingers like knives at Nicholas's mother, "This is *your* fault! Leaving him alone for hours!" Nicholas's father stormed out of the room. The front door announced his departure from the premises. That night his father didn't return and Nicholas slept in his mother's arms. Nicholas had never been a good sleeper and would wake up several times a night. That night he stayed awake for hours watching his mother sleep. His mother was the most beautiful woman he'd ever known. Like most three-year olds his mother was larger than life. He touched her long golden hair and felt the soft skin on her face, and wrapped her long arms like a blanket around him.

Nicholas's father did eventually return, and so the beatings began. As Nicholas grew so did the severity of the incidents. Five-year-old Nick knew never to look his father directly in the eyes, and he had the good sense of turning away when his father would hit him. Ready to brace for the pain that would come with each hit of his father's fist. Nick's beatings would be spun with malicious words. The words were intended to hurt as much as the hits. "*You* are the cause of all our problems in this world. Before *you* were here your mother and I had fun. No money issues, we could go out whenever we wanted. Drink whenever we wanted." Nick thought the last was a lie as his parents were always drinking.

When a fight ended it was always the same. Nick's father left the house; the slamming of the front door rang like a gong in Nick's ears. His mother would stand by the window with her favorite flower ceramic cup in her hand and Nick would walk up slowly behind her and wrap his arms around her waist. His mother would stroke his hair and give him a kiss on his forehead. They stood in silence side by side holding hands staring out the window. Nick's mother would look down at her son with tears in her eyes but no words ever came out. Her eyes were always talking to him where her mouth failed. Her eyes whispering to him, *I'm sorry for letting you down. I'm sorry I can't protect you from your father.*

Nick's mother was killed in a car accident when Nick was at the end of his fifth year—just shy of his sixth birthday. His father read Nick the hospital report went they went to identify the body. The report read: *Percent of alcohol in body was lethal. Cause of death: Car accident.* Nick's father made him look at the body of his dead mother. Nick looked at his dead mother's body and he saw something that looked like his mother, but it wasn't his mother at all. He began to cry but stopped when his father grabbed his hand. His father's hand held tight around Nick's tiny hand. Anyone watching would see a boy and his father having a close moment saying goodbye to a loved one. The attendant even got down and said to Nick before he left, "You will be okay Nick. Your father is still here. This will be hard. But your father can help you get through it." As they left, Nick turned to wave goodbye to the friendly attendant, and the body of his dead mother, and wished for death to come to him.

Unbeknownst to Nick, exactly two days before his mother death (after Nick's father had beaten him so badly his nose was broken) his mother had sent a letter to her brother David and his wife Lucille McKinley telling it all. On the day of her death the letter had arrived at her brother's house. David and Lucille were in shock. The secret of Nick, and his mother's life sentence, came out of the bag—she described it all. The beatings, the locking in the closet, the abuse that Nick's mother had watched her beautiful boy endure for years at the hands of her husband. When they received the call from the hospital about the sudden death of Nick's mother, David and Lucille immediately called the police explaining the situation. They watched and waited as Nick and his father pulled up into the driveway of their apartment. Nick got out of one side and his father the other. Within minutes Nick's father was surrounded by police, handcuffed and taken away in a cop car. The last words he yelled to Nick were: *Don't worry son. I will be back for you!*

Nick never got to see his mother's final words. They were locked away somewhere safely. However, he caught bits and pieces of her final letter in the whispers by adults around him: *only Nick deserved to be saved, after all she had been complicit in it all. She had been unable to do anything but stand by and watch the horror.* Nick only cared to remember that his mother had whispered to him the words, *I love you,* when she left house the night she died. Or perhaps he had imagined that.

Safe passage for young Nick was a long process. The State got involved. Nick spent a lot of time in court listening to adults deliberating over his fate. Nick's father would not look at him. In court Nick daydreamed that instead of his mother dying, his mother had taken him far away from the reach of his father. The court eventually gave custody to David and Lucille McKinley. His father went to jail. All of the adults in his life, the judges, his Aunt and Uncle, and their friends, promised Nick's father would never be able to hurt him again. His father's last words haunted his dreams for a full year, until Nick decided, maybe the adults could be believed. *Maybe.*

Nick moved into his Uncle and Aunt's house on Blackstone Boulevard. Nick was warm and safe but there was no love in the enormous house. His Aunt Lucille was extremely wealthy and spent most of her time traveling the world. She would bring gifts back from exotic places like a jade elephant from China for Nick. But, they were merely trinkets to feign affection. His Uncle David taught at RISD. His Uncle David did show interest in Nick. He introduced Nick to the world of Fine Art. His Uncle had the most extensive library of Art History. Nick would sit for hours in the quiet large library alone and read about how an artist named Van Gogh cut his ear off and then painted a self-portrait of it. He liked the more violent stories, as they felt more familiar to what he knew. Nick read about the art show that Hitler presented to demonstrate to the public what he considered horrible artwork, the German expressionists. Nick became a voracious reader of art books and at ten years old, at his request, The McKinley's signed Nick up for art lessons at an after school program.

Nick would wake crying almost every night, the taste of salt lingering on his tongue, and the wetness of his cheeks felt as smooth as silk—just like his mother's skin. His Uncle would show up at his bedside and talk to him about being a man, and how his father was in jail and could not hurt him any more. His Uncle would say his mother had loved him, and how Nick's face looked so much like his mother when she was young. His Uncle would say the same words every time, "Your mother is in Heaven. She is an angel and I'm sure she is looking over you Nick." The thought of his mother in Heaven as an angel hovering above him did comfort him.

Nick had never seen his Uncle cry, but one day he did. It was as if his Uncle shrunk a full foot before his very eyes. Nick thought that kind of transformation only happened in Science Fiction books. Aunt Lucille had left her husband for good. She wasn't simply going away on one of her trips. This was a trip she would never return from. For the first time in his life Nick felt a kinship with another person. Through circumstances Nick and his Uncle had been dealt a similar blow in life, the person they loved the most had left them. His Aunt Lucille had given his Uncle two months before she was putting the large house on Blackstone Boulevard for sale. Lucille had left a note for Nick too, simply to say that if he ever needed money, he should never be afraid to call. Nick threw the note in the trash as he packed his simple belongings in boxes. Nick vowed he would NEVER go to his Aunt for anything. Nick felt a sense of loyalty to his Uncle. His Uncle had not abandoned him and Nick would *never* forget that.

His Uncle could only afford a two-bedroom apartment on his salary, but Nick didn't mind. The large house on Blackstone Boulevard had always seemed to be on loan to Nick, and turns out to his Uncle as well. Nick might have enjoyed the luxury if he had been there with his own mother. Home seemed to be a pointless direction for Nick. The only home was in his heart, and a photo of his pretty mother on a sunny day holding him when he was three. So, he kept searching hoping someday he would find a home—A home that would fill the empty space in his heart.

His Uncle had purchased him a used bike, and next to drawing it was Nick's favorite activity. He loved the feeling of moving fast and free. Nick's new neighborhood and his sad brokenhearted

Uncle came with the opportunity for independence, and the freedom of discovery. Soon, he met some other boys in the neighborhood slightly older than him, who shared his love of bike riding. Nick and his friends would ride far and explore the neighborhood in Pawtucket. Nick pedaled hard to keep up with the older boys. Nick imagined on his long bike rides that his mother was at home waiting for him when he returned (like the other kids). The warm sunshine on his face and the wind blowing against him felt like hugs and kisses from Heaven.

* *

One ride they rode farther than he'd ever been, into downtown Providence. Nick felt a sense of elation and fear. They left their bikes hidden behind a trashcan behind an office building.

"Be safe here. Only homeless, drunkards, and people after dark." Said, Pete the oldest boy.

Pete was definitely the leader of their bike gang. He was tall for his age and his long blonde hair hung in his face disguising his features that would give away his true age. Pete was the oldest of the five boys at fourteen and Nick was the youngest at twelve. Nick looked eagerly at Pete for directions as to what they were going to do next. Pete pulled a brown bag and a small bottle of rubber cement from his pocket. Nick watched and paid careful attention to everything Pete did. The preparations were ceremonial. Then Pete placed his hands around the edge of the bag and lifted over his mouth and breathed in and out. Nick watched as the brown bag collapsed and blew up three times, and then Pete's smile was wide as he passed it to the boy on his left, Gary. Gary was quiet and almost as tall as Pete, so he was second in charge therefore he was next in line for the fun. Gary scared Nick sometimes. He always seemed to be talking about killing or torturing things. The other two boys Rob and Frank were nice enough but they were eager to act tough so Pete would think they were cool.

The bag finally came around to Nick, and all eyes were on him. He knew this would decide whether or not they would continue to allow him to be part of their bike gang. Nick swore after watching his parents drinking he would never drink, but he had never thought about drugs. Nick had lived such a solitary life in the mansion on Blackstone Boulevard, his only travels being inside the pages of the art books he loved so much. This was a new path opening up to Nick and he was curious where it would take him. The sensation Nick felt when he huffed the glue was nothing like he had ever experienced in real life. Nick felt like he was floating up, up, and out of his body. He laughed so hard he thought his stomach would burst. As Pete lead the group out of the alleyway and down the street. Nick felt like he was bouncing in his chucks off the springy concrete below his feet. Pete led them to a store called Hank's Tattoo shop. Pete seemed even taller as he opened the door and walked inside under a jingling bell.

The first thing Nick heard as he entered the shop was the whirring sound of the tattoo guns. There were photos of people showing off their tattoos that ran like wall paper down the long wall the length of the tattoo shop. Nick marveled at the art that filled the walls. They were like nothing he had seen in his art books.

"Hey Hank." Pete said as he strolled down the center of the shop.

Hank, the owner, was working on a Chinese dragon on the shoulder of a large man with a beard an old barber's chair. He looked up and smiled at Pete.

The other boys lined up against the front entrance. Nick followed their lead.

"Hello stranger. Your Mom knows where you are?" Pete just shrugged and turned around defiantly in a huff knocking over a shelf of Tattoo magazines on to the floor.

"What the hell? Pete! Come back here and pick that up!" Hank yelled.

Pete walked away and Nick sheepishly bent over and started placing the magazines back on the shelf.

"Thanks." Hank replied.

"Let's leave, Nick." Pete commanded. The other boys were quickly heading out the door.

Hank glanced at Nick and asked. "What's your name kid?"

"Nick," he answered.

Hank turned back to his tattooing and replied, "Nice to meet you Nick."

As Nick turned to leave he saw Pete pocketing a couple items of jewelry from the front counter. Pete looked at him and smiled and moved his lips to say, *don't say anything.*

Pete was out the front door. Nick walked slowly wondering if he should tell Hank and risk losing his friends, or let it go. He felt conflicted. He felt guilty. Nick stopped at the front desk where a pile of postcards with Hank's creations sat on a spinning tray.

"Excuse me Hank. Could I take one of these?" Nick asked. "*Really* amazing artwork."

Hank stared at Nick for another second. Nick let a sense of dread creep up inside him. A million thoughts flew through his head: *Hank knew about what Pete did. Hank thinks I am part of the cover up. He thinks I am trying to get away with this. He braced himself as he had when his father would lay a punch on him. He was a bad kid and he deserved it.* But instead Hank smiled and replied "Of course." Then paused, and said, "You seem like a nice kid, Nick. Watch out for Pete. That kid isn't always right in the head."

"Thank you sir." Nick said nervously and slipped the postcard into his back pocket. Out on the street the boys were gone. Nick looked around and just as he was about to give up, he caught sight of them across the street one block away turning down another street. Nick ran to catch up with the rest of the boys. Pete was busy pulling out something out of his backpack. The boys were huddled around so closely Nick couldn't see what they were marveling over.

"Thought we'd lost you Nick." said Pete.

Suddenly, Pete seemed even taller than before and much older than his fourteen years. Something in Pete's voice reminded him of his father. It had a sinister undertone.

"We are going to shoot some fireworks off onto the river when the river boats go by. You're first. You hit a boat you're in. You hit the water you're out."

Before Nick knew what was happening, Pete handed him a firework and they snuck down under a bridge crossing. They hid under the bridge and laid down flat in the grass. Pete lit the firecracker and ran away. Nick stayed low and waited for Pete's whistle to tell him the boat was going to be passing under the bridge. Everything moved slowly at first. Nick felt like his breathing was echoing under the bridge and he would surely be caught. It was exciting and horrifying at the same time. The firecracker was burning closer to his hand, and if he didn't chuck it soon his hand would be burned pretty badly. Then it was as if time sped up, the whistle from Pete came, the boat arrived with people looking overboard smiling. He chucked the firework and closed his eyes and ran for his life. He heard a *bang, bang, bang!!!* Behind his closed eyes he imagined the damage the shot could take and his father's face appeared alongside it. Behind him screaming and chaos and Nick prayed he hadn't hit a baby in a mother's arms. Nick ran so fast that he didn't notice passing the rest of the boys hiding behind a car. He started to slow down as he heard a burst of laughter and yells of, "Nick! You can stop running now!"

Nick turned around and saw Pete and the other boys laughing at him, and he stood his ground for a moment, thinking about Hank's warning in the tattoo shop. "Man, I think you put a hole in that boat!" Gary added, "Yeah, I think I saw an arm floating in the water!" Nick paused in disbelief, not being able to think about the destruction he had caused. It must have showed on his face, because Pete hit him over the head, and asked, "What's the matter, dummy?" Nick, acted quickly, began to laugh it off, and the other boys joined. Nick didn't know if they were laughing with him or at him. There was a moment he thought about walking away, but soon they were celebrating Nick and talking about how brave he was. Nick *wanted* to belong somewhere. Nick *wanted* to be a part of this gang.

All summer Nick and the other boys rode their bikes around Pawtucket and Providence pulling pranks, spraying graffiti and committing a few minor crimes. For the first time in his life Nick thought perhaps he had found his home. Hank had also opened a new door for Nick. When he wasn't hanging out with the boys, Nick helped out at the tattoo shop. Nick would help get things from the stockroom like cotton balls, jars of Vaseline, or rubbing alcohol, and in return Nick was allowed to use drawing paper to draw. Nick loved drawing in Hank's shop, as there was so much to be inspired by. The place was like a living art gallery. Nick studied the human form, animals, anything that was real and not real. Hank would help him when he had trouble with the perspective or a shape, and hence Nick's art lessons continued in a very unorthodox place.

When Nick turned thirteen his Uncle suggested he get a job after school to keep him out of trouble. his Uncle made remarks from time to time about "those boys he hung out with." It seemed like Hank agreed because one day when Nick was leaving the tattoo shop, Hank handed him two twenty dollar bills and said, "I figured it was about time I paid you for all that work you've been doing for me." So Nick was officially in charge of the stock room, making appointments, and cleaning the place.

On Nick's days off from work in the summer and weekends, the morning routine was clear. Throwing fireworks at the mail truck with the boys stopped for no one and nothing, except Siobhan. Siobhan was fourteen, from California. A tan, beach blonde, a movie star placed miraculously by some luck to THEIR block in Pawtucket? Siobhan would appear in the early morning on the front steps of her building, eating a breakfast donut and reading a comic book. Being the pack leader Pete was the first to talk to her. Nick's window faced the front of the building and he could see Pete and Siobhan talking. Pete looked goofy as he tried acting cool and impressing the new blonde girl from California. Siobhan looked back down at the comic book in her hand and repositioned her extensive collection of bangles that hung from her slim wrist.

Soon the other boys showed up and while Pete looked annoyed, Siobhan seemed to be enjoying the new round of adulation that surrounded her. Not wanting to be left out Nick made his way down and sat quietly on a nearby step. He was the farthest from Siobhan, but as far as he was concerned he was fine with that. Her beauty made him nervous. Nick stared down at the sidewalk and

noticed a rogue comic book that had fallen off of Siobhan's stack of comic books. Pulling out a pencil from his back pocket, he began to redraw the characters in the margins. Siobhan quickly noticed Nick's defamation of her favorite comic book jumped up and grabbed the pencil out Nick's hand. Nick startled, looked up for the first time revealing to Siobhan his handsome blue eyes. Siobhan smiled coyly, suddenly realizing she'd insulted the cutest boy in the neighborhood. The stare was interrupted by a knock on the head from Pete and he yelled, "Come on stupid! It's time to fucking go!"

One evening Nick was sitting outside finishing a drawing under the street light when a slight shadow came across the white of the page. He looked up and Siobhan was two feet away.

"Hey, that's a pretty neat drawing." She said leaning in closer to see. "May I join you?" she said, after sitting next to him and pulling his drawing pad over on to her lap.

Siobhan smelled liked a mixture of sugar and suntan lotion. Nick surprised himself by thinking about how much he wanted to be around her. At first, they spent nights talking on the steps while Nick drew. Soon the focus of Nick's drawings became Siobhan and the conversation became playful. Several weeks later Siobhan kissed Nick. It was the most wonderful thing Nick had ever experienced—infinitely better than huffing glue or riding a bike. He felt like he was in Heaven. Siobhan's kisses were soft and tasted as sweet as they smelled. A week later word got around that Nick and Siobhan were an item. Hearing Pete laughing at the back of his head Nick began to feel divided in two. Pete and the boys were waiting for him. Nick knew he could only avoid them for so long. The tattoo shop became his hideaway, and Hank, his confidant.

Nick poured out all his worries about losing his friendship with Pete and the boys, and how Siobhan hated them, to Hank. Nick talked about how he felt torn. Nick spoke about how safe he felt with Siobhan, and how he felt he could tell her anything. Nick talked about how he loved that she would laugh with him and not at him. Siobhan made him feel free. Hank listened patiently and wholeheartedly to the young boy's troubles.

"She always asks me, why I would want to hang out with people who were so mean to me?" Nick told Hank.

Hank said to Nick, "Maybe *she* is right."

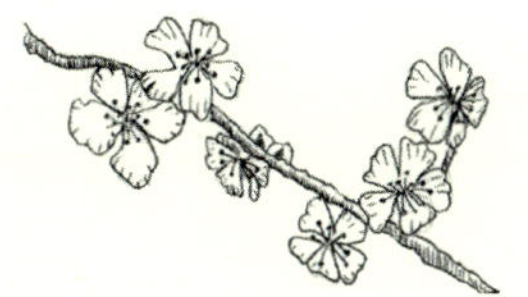

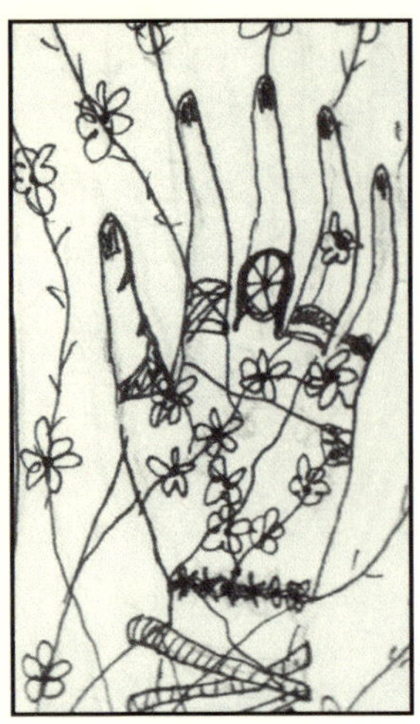

Every Good Artist Needs a Muse

Everyone looked at Raina as if she were the most unusual flower. There are moths and there are butterflies. Moths appear only when there is a light to attract them. Butterflies, however, make their own light by attracting it out of the people around them. See a butterfly and you become a child. Raina was a butterfly with a million colors. She flew in to Providence one day and no one knows from where. Raina was a muse. When she met an artist, she made jewelry happen, and made paintings happen. When she walked into a room, she made the party happen. When Raina wore deep red lipstick, the following night, everyone wore deep red lipstick. This was true for when she wore feathers on her eyelashes and orchids in her hair.

Raina had as many jobs as she had friends. She seemed to be everywhere at once. Most of the time she worked in the vintage boutique called *Orange Flowers and Things* on Broadway near her apartment. Raina used to shop there for her clothes and then one day the owner of the shop, Daisy, offered her a job. Ever since Raina had been in the shop, Daisy marveled at how sales had doubled. Raina wasn't a great sales person per say, she just had conversations with customers about the clothing and while giving them a tour of the shop was able to help the customer find what they wanted. Like a butterfly she would flit around the customers like they were flowers, and somehow make them feel special.

Raina was always in motion. When there were no customers she busied herself straightening the clothes, making sure the manequins looked good, and rearranging display areas. Raina turned music on loud enough to help her with the work but not too loud to scare the customers away. When customers wandered into the boutique someone would *always* ask Raina what was playing on the stereo. This happened all the time. Raina listened to the most underground music. When a friend in a band didn't give her free music to listen to, a customer inevitably did. Most of the time it was because bands on tour came to shop at the boutique and would hand her a copy of their music. Daisy was amazed that not only would people leave the store with bags of clothes and jewelry from Raina, they would always leave Raina with something. Daisy only wished Raina would work more, but at every offer of more employment Raina simply said, "Oh, Daisy, I wish I had more time. You know I *love* working here. Thank you for thinking of me."

A day in the life of Raina was filled with magic, surprises, and paths that curved like roots of a tree. They intertwined so thick it was hard to know where one path started and where one path ended. She went to sleep at nine am and got up at one pm.

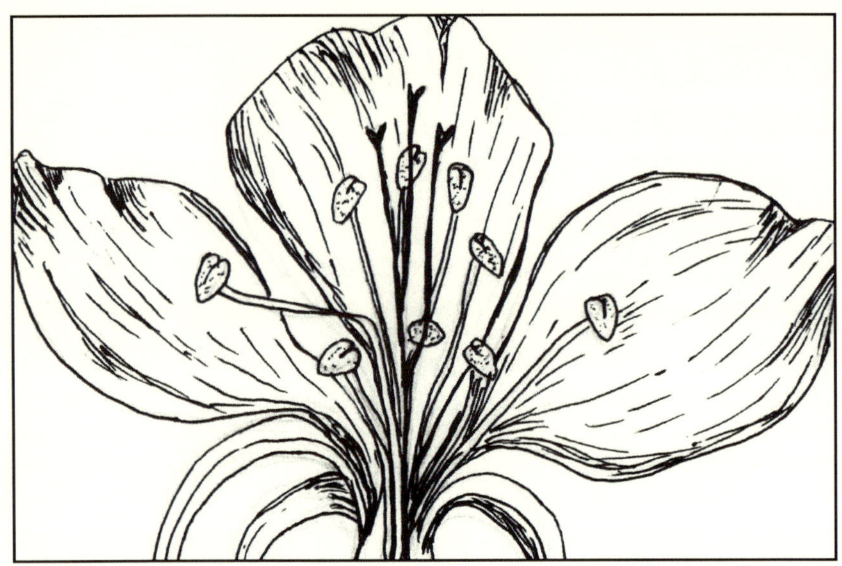

This gave her enough time to grab some coffee, a croissant, and walk to work. Work meant the boutique, a coffee shop, or an occasional catering for some fabulous event, which always turned into a late night party. Every day Raina took off her sleeping mask, jumped in the shower, reapplied her favorite deep red lipstick and and let chance circumstance run the direction of her day.

On a humid day in June, a woman in worn jeans and a well-loved t-shirt seemed to be struggling to find something on the racks. Raina could always spot trouble in the boutique and her mission was to make it go away. Raina quickly sized the woman in trouble as, 5'7", mid thirties, and a tough chick. Away Raina flitted around the store gathering a pile of clothes she had specifically chosen for the woman in trouble. Raina was never pushy. It was always like an easy conversation with what felt like an old friend. Raina walked over to the lady and said a quick "hello."

The woman looked up and said, "hey" in a raspy voice.

"Wow! Where did you get those boots?" Raina asked genuinely stooping down to the floor to get a better look. The woman had cowboy boots with red and yellow painted flowers creeping up the sides and into the handles.

The woman laughed, and said, "These old things? Nashville. Had them for a long time. They've traveled almost as far as I have."

"I'm Raina," She said standing up and shaking hands with the woman.

"Joan." The woman replied with a smile.

"Hey, I'm no expert but these pants look like they would fit you perfectly." Raina said handing the black leather pants she had in the pile of clothes in her hands.

"These are cool. Thanks." Joan replied taking them. "I'll try them on."

"Great! Let's have a look." Raina said with a smile, sitting on a wrought iron bench across from the dressing rooms, with her legs crossed.

"Oh. *Now?*" Joan asked. A big smile spread across her face. "You know, that's the first time someone has asked me that in, well, *forever.*"

"How come?" Raina asked.

"I buy clothes for other people." Joan laughed.

"Well, give me those other things you found and get in that dressing booth!" Raina directed.

Within ten minutes Raina had given Joan a mini makeover. At the cash register Joan paid Raina. Then Joan handed

Raina some tickets and backstage VIP passes to Black Sabbath at the PPAC. Turned out Joan was the costume designer for Black Sabbath. Raina took the tickets and thanked Joan, saying simply "Thanks! That really is too generous. But thanks!" Raina closed the shop and headed to the coffee shop White Electric for a quick dinner. It was en route to her apartment, and since she worked there too, she got free food. As she approached her friend Nick Shelby was sitting on the bench out front.

"Hey Nick." Raina said giving him a hug and a kiss on the cheek, "What's happening?"

"Leaving tonight to go to Japan." Nick said, "You want anything?"

"Japan. That's right! Wow. You must be *so* excited! Wow. Japan. Man, a year ago AS220, now Japan! I'm so proud of you Nick!" Raina exclaimed.

"Yeah, pretty cool, my first solo show in Japan. I never thought this day would happen to me." Nick said humbly.

"Oh come on! *I* did! *All* of us did." Raina said.

The two sat quietly in a moment of silence.

Nick, you ready for this ride?" Raina asked, "I keep thinking about Stan."

They were both silent. But it wasn't an awkward silence, just a thoughtful one.

"Stan was *so* good. You seen him lately?" Nick said with a sigh.

"Now and then. He's not good. He came begging at the boutique and Daisy called the police on him. I wasn't in that day. I *wish* I had been, but what do you say?" Raina said. She fidgeted with a pink costume ring on her index finger. "Stan gave this to me."

"I remember." Nick said. "You *really* loved him Raina. I'm so sorry."

"I do. I mean I did. Sometimes." Raina's voice dropped. "Promise me you will *never* do heroine, Nick." Raina said pushing away a tear.

Nick put his arm around Raina. Raina leaned her head against Nick's shoulder. They were good friends. They sat in a comfortable silence staring at the sky.

"Strange to think you'll be up there soon heading to Japan. I'm proud of you Nick. *Really.*" Raina finished as she glanced up at the sky.

"Thanks Raina. That means a lot." Nick smiled. "Guess what came in the mail today?"

"Raina smiled and looked at Nick, "It did? How much Nick?"

"Let's just say more money than *I've* ever had. Shit, one piece from a rich lady in LA? Crazy, *right?*" Nick asked.

"That reminds me. You won't believe what *I* got at work today" Raina said smiling. "Guess Nick. Guess." Raina teased.

"I think it's easier to guess what you didn't get." Nick laughed.

Raina gave Nick a friendly punch.

"What? Come on Raina. It's just hard to keep track sometimes. People are *always* giving you things." Nick continued. "Well deserved, of course."

"Yeah. I have no idea why! But check this out. Are you

ready for this? This lady gave me backstage passes to meet Black Sabbath, the whole original lineup." Raina said pulling them out of her bag to show Nick.

"What the fuck! Let me see!" Nick said checking the tickets and badges. "Wow. How? What's the story?"

Raina responded coyly "I dunno! I just helped a lady with an outfit. Turns out she works for Black Sabbath."

They both laughed and took some selfies with the tickets in their hands until Nick's phone bleeped a text. "Oh shit! I gotta go and pack. That was my reminder." Nick said getting up. They hugged each other hard.

"Bring me back something cool." Raina said.

"I will." Nick replied and walked away.

Raina headed into the coffee shop and ordered dinner: a raspberry scone, from her friend Bryce behind the counter.

"Hey Raina, I'm djing tonight at Warehouse 9. You should come and bring some friends. I'll put you on the list, plus five." Bryce said handing her food.

"Cool. Thanks." Raina said. Bryce blushed.

When Raina turned onto Broadway toward her apartment, she noticed the street was blocked. There were movie trailers everywhere. She stood there pondering an alternate route when her friend Clay texted her: *Wes Anderson movie on ur street*

She texted back: *right here now*

At that moment Raina looked up to see a man with a big black walkie-talkie in his hands. The mysterious man asked her if she'd stand in as an extra for the next scene. "Yeah, sure why not. That sounds like fun."

"I promise it won't take more than fifteen minutes. I'm Jim, set manager." The man said smiling at her and holding out his hand.

Raina shook his hand.

Conceding, she said "Oh, no worries," And just like that, she was on set, getting her face done, and then quickly putting a paisley mini-dress on her. Fifteen minutes later, as promised, she was done. She only saw Wes standing behind the camera. That was as close as Raina got. She snuck a picture when he wasn't looking. Jim thanked Raina for her time. As she got ready to leave, she said to the set manager, "Wait, I'm still wearing your dress."

"Just keep it," the man shouted after her, "You look beautiful in it."

"Hey, by the way," he carried on, "What's there to do around here at night? The crew wants to go out." Already almost a block away, Raina shouted back "Warehouse 9. Bryce is Djing. It'll be great. Come."

As Raina was putting her key into the door of her apartment building, her phone rang. It was her friend Petra asking, "Where are you Raina? I'm freaking out. I *need* you, babe. My jewelry show."

"Oh shit! I'm so sorry! Fuck! I'm on way now! I am such an asshole! I love you!" Realizing she was already dressed and made up, Raina hopped in a cab and headed to Petra's jewelry show. The jewelry show was in was the most exclusive show in Providence. Petra had been accepted and this was a real honor, and Raina being a good friend could not miss it. Very wealthy people were going to be buying Petra's jewelry tonight. When Raina arrived, The Providence Business Journal was interviewing Petra in a booth by the front window of the gallery. Raina smiled and waved at her friend Petra and found the catering table for a glass of white wine, and cheese and crackers.

Suddenly Petra was by her side, "Raina, the photographer wants to take a picture of you wearing the piece I made for you. I mentioned it."

Raina locked arms with Petra, and soon found herself talking about her friend Petra and the cameras were snapping pictures of the two of them smiling.

"What an exquisite piece." the reporter said pointing to Raina's neck.

Petra responded, "I made this piece for Raina. Actually, I made this piece because of Raina."

"I don't know if it's the wine, but I feel like I'm going to cry." Raina said. The photographer snapped a last shot and said thank you.

"I'm so proud of you Petra!" Raina said, "And thanks honey. I mean *really*. What you said in the interview."

Their special moment was interrupted by a text from her boarding school friends Jake and Paul that they were having dinner down the street and Raina should join them.

"Honey, I got to run. Jake and Paul invited me to dinner." Raina said. "Think I need to call a cab?"

"I can give you a ride. It's on my way home. Let me just pack up." Petra said.

Raina looked at ease eating duck confit and drinking Bordeaux—all at the expense of her rich friends. They always refused to let her pay for anything. In return, Raina always made sure they had a fun night. When they asked what was on the plans for the evening Raina said, "Warehouse 9. Bryce is djing!" The Black Sabbath tickets would not be enticing for this group. She would have to wait and see who would be interested as the night proceeded. The check was paid and soon they were zipping down the street in her friend Jake's Mercedes and headed to Olneyville.

Warehouse 9 was a large building with a main dance floor and a series of smaller side rooms that blasted the music that was coming out of the main room. Each room had a different theme. In the black room where everything glowed, Raina lost her boarding school friends and ran into her friends Jackie and Audrey. Raina, Jackie, and Audrey made the rounds beginning in the day glow room where your teeth were harrowing white and the floors were painted in neon swirls that vibrated under your feet. Next, the Sixties room which was all white with shag carpet and dancing cages. To the Madhouse room with six different levels all at varying angles so you had to move about the room like a pinball in a pinball machine. Finally, the Funhouse Room with mirrors on the walls and floors. Raina's reflection was like a Shiva with a million arms that reflected everywhere in the Funhouse Room. Raina loved to dance and she loved the feeling of getting lost and sweating. Soon she was drenched and feeling the buzz of endorphins rushing to her brain. Eventually, the wine and coffee and her busy schedule had caught up with her, and Raina was forced to take a bathroom break. Jackie and Audrey followed along to freshen up. Raina pulled out her favorite lipstick and the VIP tickets to the concert fell out of her purse. "Oh shit! I totally forgot about this! Shit! What time is it?"

"It's midnight." Audrey said looking at her phone. "You got tickets to Black Sabbath???"

"I bet they are still onstage." Raina said excitedly. "Either of you drive here tonight?"

"Jackie did. Can we come please??" Audrey and Jackie screamed at the same time.

Raina smiled wildly and danced. Then said, "Let's go!" Jackie and Audrey were exactly the people she had been waiting to share this amazing gift with.

Raina, Jackie, and Audrey arrived to see the encore and then head backstage to meet Black Sabbath. Jackie and Audrey took a million pictures backstage. Raina and Joan hung out, and Raina got the official introduction and photo ops with the band. As their tour bus was packing up to leave, Raina got goodbye hugs from all, and Joan and Raina traded cell numbers. Within no time Raina, Audrey, and Jackie were back at Warehouse 9 showing off where they had been with Raina.

As Raina entered each room, everyone couldn't believe that she had been to meet Black Sabbath and now was back. It seemed like Raina had been there all the time, as if she left a trail of tracings everywhere she stepped. They had only been gone for an hour and half. They stayed until Warehouse 9 closed but the party continued at Bryce's house and as the sun came up he made everyone breakfast. At seven in the morning, Raina moved the beer bottles off the sink and into the trash barrel. Raina stared into the mirror, washed her face and reapplied a thick coat of deep red lipstick. "Let's do it again," she whispered to herself and blew a kiss and headed to greet the new day.

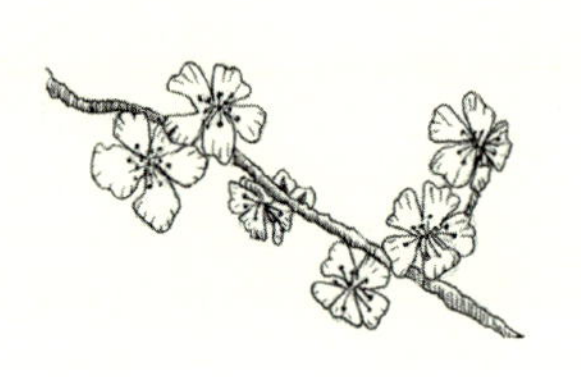

You Must Accept Me, RISD

You must accept me, thought Audrey. Jackie and Audrey, two teen punks, sat on a short brick wall across from the Museum of The Rhode Island School of Design (also known as RISD), deep in thought. The brick college buildings lined the block like stately soldiers from another era. The street was eerily empty of people, cars, and any life whatsoever. That was Providence. One minute filled with life, the next like an apocalypse had hit. The trees were bare and wet leaves were pasted everywhere imaginable, sidewalk, steps, gutter, windows, and streets. A raw cold wind came and went occasionally lifting leaves and placing them elsewhere.

You *must* accept me," whispered Audrey with pink hair, black motorcycle jacket, and rust color combat boots—pointing her lit cigarette in the direction of the museum, squinting her eyes tight.

"You *must* accept me. You *must* accept me," said Jackie,

with blue-black hair, checkered coat, and eyes closed—cigarette out in front of her commandingly.

The brick wall ran half the block in either direction of where the two girls sat. Behind the wall a small courtyard of trees and benches were layered in four tiers. An inviting place for a student to sit and enjoy some outdoors between classes, but on this cold wet day it was empty. Jackie picked off a wet stack of discolored leaves from the bottom of her boots and tossed them to the ground. Audrey smoked nervously on her cigarette and alternately bit at her raw cuticles that were already well worn away from habitual biting. A cold smoky air cloaked the girls in the early winter chill. Jackie placed her cigarette on the wall and pulled on some fingerless gloves. Jackie picked up her cigarette and leaned back to look at the sky.

"Lovely weather we are having." Jackie said into the air with a smile.

Jackie's statement had the effect of pulling Audrey out of her self induced tortured state. Audrey relaxed into a smile and stubbed her cigarette out. Audrey pulled a mugger black hat out of her pocket and slid it over her head with a shiver. Audrey's hazel eyes wandered back in the direction of the museum building across the street as if the building held some magnetic power. The brick and ivy walls lay behind a wrought iron gate with a small courtyard. Audrey knew every inch of what lay behind the stately entrance of the RISD Museum. Jackie and Audrey had spent a lot of time following along with the tours pretending they were RISD students. There was a rare Hellenistic bronze Aphrodite. The Egyptian collection had an amazing Ptolemaic period coffin and even a mummy. In the Contemporary Art wing there was Roy Lichtenstein and Andy Warhol. Audrey had memorized the names. They were keys to her future. Knowledge is power.

"You think *every* artist thinks about wanting to be accepted? You think Andy Warhol cared?" Audrey asked.

"Does what? Begs to be accepted by RISD?" Jackie replied smiling with eyebrows raised.

"No, I mean, feel the *need* to be accepted?" Audrey asked, "*God!* It makes me feel so, so . . . *desperate!*"

Audrey pulled her legs up to her chin and looked like a little kid pouting. Audrey took her stubbed out cigarette and began to draw a series of black patterns on the brick surface of the wall with a nervous energy.

"Every artist desires an audience. Every artist wants to be noticed, appreciated, and admired." Jackie replied with authority of an old wise Zen master.

"*Every* single one of them?" Audrey asked, now fully consumed by her anxiety again and biting her cuticles.

Jackie simply nodded her head and looked wise as she lit a fresh cigarette. She blew out the first puff and leaned back and looked at the sky. "Artists are consumed by the need to always seek satisfaction, and yet *never* to be satisfied." Jackie said as if she was in a trance. Audrey eagerly awaited Jackie's next words of wisdom, but Jackie remained quiet for a long time.

Jackie was silent for so long, that Audrey stopped looking at Jackie and turned her attention to a girl with long hair passing by who had appeared as if out of nowhere. The girl walked with ease and comfort with her black portfolio at her side.

"Then it's NYC baby. It's inevitable. Everyone who goes to RISD does." Jackie's voice snapped Audrey back to reality.

"God! I *HAVE* to get into RISD!" Audrey said. Audrey held out an unlit cigarette closed her eyes and resumed her chanting: *You must accept me! You must accept me* in an audible whisper. She closed her eyes and for the first time all day looked completely focused and relaxed. Audrey *could* see herself at RISD, she *could* see herself in New York, and it made Audrey smile.

"What are you smiling about Audrey?" Jackie asked.

"New York. Cool. I can see myself there. Totally." Audrey said. "Just sometimes, I don't feel like an artist because I feel like I want it so badly. I mean a true artist wouldn't feel so desperate like I do, right?"

"No. They *all* do. Why do you think famous artists are so screwed up?" Jackie said, "Fame and money doesn't change that. These things are just hidden inside them. *Trust me.* They don't want to talk about it is all. Ruin their reputation. It's why famous people can't stay out of the news. Crashing cars, getting married over and over again, you know stupid stuff. Acceptance. *That's* what they are seeking." Jackie finished definitively as if the conversation was closed for discussion.

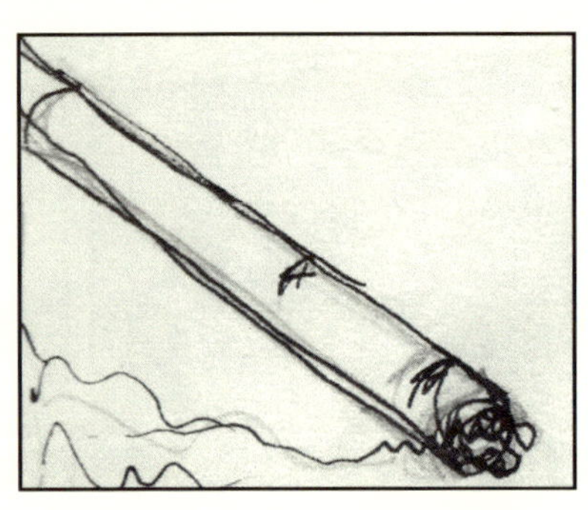

"YOU *MUST* ACCEPT ME! YOU *MUST* ACCEPT ME!" Audrey shouted suddenly, the scream releasing all her previous anxiousness. "God! That felt good!"

A few students, as if dropped from the sky, appeared in front of them walking by with black portfolios. As they passed they glanced at Audrey briefly as they continued on their way with a look of disdain and annoyance.

"YOU *MUST* ACCEPT ME! YOU *MUST* ACCEPT ME!" Audrey shouted even louder. Now standing on the wall acting like the tough punk she was dressed as.

"Freaks." A student in a black leather jacket mumbled as he passed Audrey and Jackie, continuing to strut down the sidewalk with a swagger of a rock star walking up to the microphone.

Suddenly, Jackie stood up on the wall next to Audrey and shouted as loud as she could to the guy, "Fuck you! *We* are artists! And, *We* live here! *We* are not just visiting!"

Jackie jumped down and motioned to Audrey to follow suit. They broke off in a manic run down the block. Jackie and Audrey both shouted, "Go back to Connecticut!!!" —with middle fingers up, running down the street and laughing. They ran as fast as they could through a sudden crowd of RISD students that had just exited one of the buildings. Jackie and Audrey knocked a few students supplies on to the ground, but didn't stop to apologize. When they were out of sight of the RISD students, Jackie and Audrey stopped to catch their breath; laughing so hard they almost fell down. Jackie leaned against the wall of an old building with ivy leaves and spread her arms out wide.

"Jackie, watch out." Audrey said pulling Jackie off the wall. "Look! The fountain." She said.

In front of Jackie and Audrey was a fountain shaped like a large clamshell surrounded by several arches with varying patterns and the date 1873 etched into the granite at the top of the structure. Everyone said that if you drink from this particular fountain you would never leave Providence. Local folklore. Coincidentally it was in front of a building known as The Athenaeum, a favorite haunt of the infamous authors of gothic horror Edgar Allen Poe and H.P. Lovecraft.

"Take a picture of me looking like I'm drinking from it, and I'll fix it on the computer later and make it look like I'm drinking from it." Jackie said.

Audrey snapped a few pictures on her phone. Suddenly, 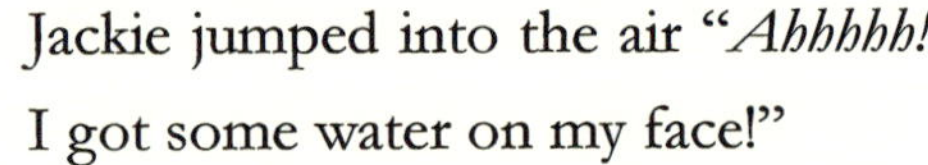
Jackie jumped into the air "*Ahhhhh!* I got some water on my face!"

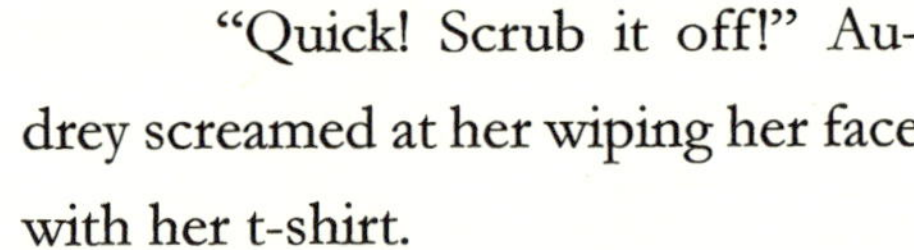
"Quick! Scrub it off!" Audrey screamed at her wiping her face with her t-shirt.

Then Jackie and Audrey's heads simultaneously tilted towards the sky and above the top of the fountain's back wall. The building behind the fountain now consumed them both. All thoughts of being stuck in Providence as old maids dissipated from their thoughts and curiosity gleamed in both girls' eyes. At the angle the girls were standing the building looked immense against the dark grey sky. Two black wrought iron lanterns jutted out on the ends of the last row of steps leading to the front door. Two long columns held a pediment reminiscent of Greek Architecture.

“You know, I’ve always wanted to go into that building.” Jackie said her blue eyes gleaming.

“Me too.” Audrey replied.

Jackie and Audrey slowly walked along the short wrought iron fence that wrapped the building. The black spikes felt cold under their fingertips as they touched the tips and made their way to the little swinging gate. Jackie opened the small old-fashioned gate and they both walked along a short path to the large wide stone steps. They paused momentarily to admire the building at a closer range. It looked even more impressive as it towered above them. Jackie and Audrey walked side by side up the main steps each unable to resist touching one of the two lampposts that flanked the steps of the entrance. Jackie pulled the heavy iron door at the top of the steps.

They both walked inside and stopped a few feet in. It was dead quiet. The smell of old books lingered in the air. There was no one inside the building, not even a librarian. On the ceiling were strips of glass that let in dusty light that spread around the endless layers of books and shelves that spanned out in every direction from where they stood. They moved around touching the books and wandering through the shelves of books. A shiny golden bust eventually drew them both back to the same spot. The plaque read *H.P. Lovecraft.* Audrey and Jackie stood mesmerized. Neither girl said a word but they looked at each other and knew exactly what each other was thinking. Jackie and Audrey both loved the folklore of Providence, and H.P. Lovecraft was at the top of the list.

“You know, they say, his ghost visits this place often.” A

voice from behind them made them both start.

They turned around to see an older man with grey hair, a tweed suit, and an H.P. Lovecraft book against his chest a few feet from where they stood. He had translucent blue eyes that shone behind his wire frame glasses. He didn't smile. Even Jackie was so startled she didn't spit out one of her usual quips.

"You girls need any assistance?" He said looking them both directly in the eyes.

The man's blue eyes were mesmerizing. There was something about them that held your gaze and froze you in your place. Both girls said nothing. The light above faded and the room suddenly felt dark and cold.

"You girls don't speak?" The man said with eyebrows raised. His blue eyes seemed as if they were lit from behind.

Jackie started nudging Audrey to move sideways, and quickly said, "No. We are all set. Thanks. Looking for a specific book."

Jackie then pulled Audrey into the end of the row of bookshelves and out of sight of the strange man.

"What the fuck was that about." Jackie whispered.

"I know what a freak." Audrey replied.

They both peeked around the corner and the man was still there staring at the H.P. Lovecraft bust with the book in his hands. He slowly turned his head in their direction as if he sensed the girls' presence. Jackie and Audrey slid back against the bookshelves. *Creepy* Jackie mouthed to Audrey. Audrey led the way this time and they slid quietly down the row until they got to the end of the row. They ducked down low as to avoid any possibly viewing from the strange man. They ran across to the next row of shelves to hide and catch their breath.

"Do you think he saw us?" whispered Jackie.

"I don't think so," whispered Audrey.

"Why the *hell* did we come in here?" Jackie whispered.

They heard the sound of heavy feet walking in their direction. Both girls stood as still as they could. The feet stopped around the corner a few feet from where the girls were sitting. *BAM! BAM! BAM!* Echoed around them like a gunshot.

BAM! BAM! BAM!

Jackie and Audrey clutched at each other.

"What the fuck!" Jackie whispered into Audrey's ear.

Audrey held Jackie tight.

Then there was dead silence.

SCREECHHHH! SCREECH! The footsteps started up again and moved right to the edge of where the girls sat and then stopped.

The girls held each other as tight as they possibly could.

The footsteps started again but they were moving away from them.

"Let's move Jackie." Audrey whispered and pulled Jackie up.

Audrey peeked around the corner and saw the back of the man in the tweed suit.

"Quick!" Audrey whispered and pulled Jackie to the next row of shelves.

Audrey peeked around the next corner and saw the man turn his head slowly to the side. He remained standing still like a statue. To the left of the man she saw an exit sign. Audrey and Jackie wove in an out of the bookshelves to get closer to the exit. The footsteps recommenced and seemed to be just around each corner from where the girls found a new place to hide. Audrey peaked around the corner. To her surprise this time she saw a woman with glasses working on a computer at the main desk.

"Jackie, someone else is here. Look." Audrey whispered to Jackie.

"I can't take this. *Why* did I bring us in here!" Jackie whispered to Audrey. She looked like she was about to cry.

Audrey was shocked. She'd never Jackie in this state. Suddenly it was as if roles had reversed. Audrey felt that she had to be brave for Jackie, after all Jackie had done it for her so many times. This was her turn to pay Jackie back.

"Let's go over to her." Audrey said standing up and motioning to Jackie to follow suit.

Jackie remained seated and fixed in her place. Jackie refused to budge. Audrey peeked around the corner to see if the woman was actually there, or if it had merely been a figment of her imagination. There the lady was working away. The room had darkened and the light from the woman's computer cast a glow on the woman's face. Audrey slowly walked toward her. The woman looked up as Audrey stood in front of her desk.

"Can I help you?" the woman asked.

Audrey hadn't prepared for what she wanted to say to the woman. She knew it would sound crazy to ask the woman if there was a ghost that haunted The Athenaeum. Audrey stood silent feeling dumb. Luckily, the woman asked another question.

"Is there a book you are looking for? I am Ms. Lamb the librarian here." She said with a smile.

"*Ahh.* Yes. H.P. Lovecraft." Audrey sputtered out.

"Any specific book?" Ms. Lamb asked.

Audrey shook her head.

"Well, we have so many. Let me show you the Lovecraft section." Ms. Lamb said getting up from her desk and heading over towards where Jackie was hiding.

Ms. Lamb started pointing out books to Audrey. Audrey saw Jackie peek around the corner to see if it was safe. Audrey waved her to come. Jackie got up and walked over to them and said, "*The Call of Cthulhu* is awesome!"

Ms. Lamb shrieked at the sound of Jackie's voice.

"Oh my lord child. Don't go sneaking up on old ladies like that. You might kill them." Ms. Lamb said clutching at her chest.

"Sorry M'am, I'm here with her." Jackie said as her cheeks flushed red.

Ms. Lamb shook her head and walked away.

Jackie and Audrey looked at each other.

"Let's get out of here." Jackie said.

"Agreed." Audrey said.

They walked passed the woman's desk and said "Thank you, Ms. Lamb."

Ms. Lamb looked up at them and shook her head and mumbled something about kids today.

Jackie pushed open the heavy iron door and a blast of cold air welcomed them into the dark afternoon.

"That was freaky." Jackie said.

Audrey shook her head and lit a cigarette. Jackie did the same. They sat down on the bottom step and sat silently breathing the cold air in deeply between puffs.

"Heard that Hannah's band Sister Eleven is playing tonight. Want to dye our hair a new color for the show?" Jackie asked. Audrey smiled.

In an instant the mood had lightened.

"Can I have a light?" a voice came from the side path.

Audrey and Jackie stood up to see whom the voice belonged to. It was none other than the same old man who had been inside the building.

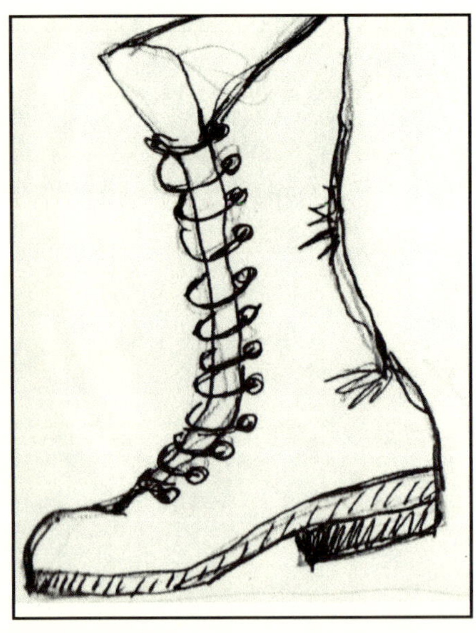

Jackie didn't stop to answer. She grabbed Audrey's arm and dragged her and ran past the man. Jackie flung open the small black gate in front of her. The two teenagers ran as fast as they could up the long winding hill adjacent to the building. It seemed like the hill went on forever. They didn't stop running until they hit crowded Thayer Street—far away from the haunted library. Jackie and Audrey stood on the corner to catch their breath. As more people passed, they felt the comfort of the safety of being in a crowd. They looked at each other and then began laughing hysterically. The range of emotions they had felt that day had to be released. After all, they were only teenagers. Soon, they walked arm and arm singing their favorite song by their favorite band *Sister Eleven.* They stopped in front of Providence Comics. Jackie opened the door and they were greeted by the sounds of distorted guitars and other teenagers just like them.

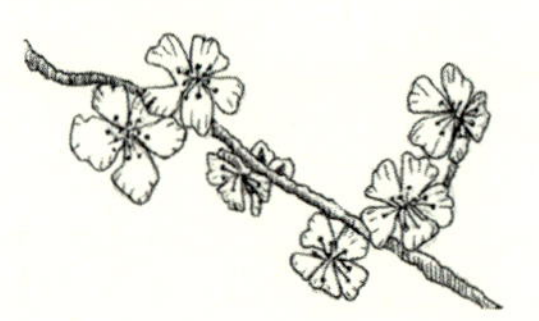

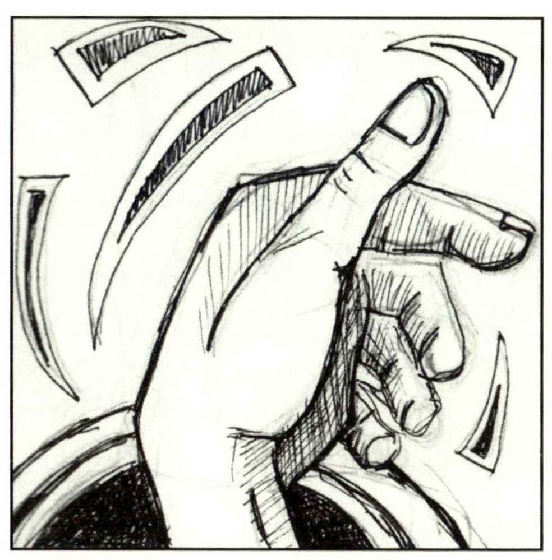

The Invisible Boy Creates Something

He sat quietly through every class. He was invisible to the students around him. Sometimes The Invisible Boy was so quiet the teachers even forget he was there. Most of the time he slipped into a daydream of lines, shapes and forms. The Invisible Boy imagined the words and noises escaping the mouths of the other humans in the room around him as clouds, trees, or maybe a bird. To him letters had always looked like objects, *not* letters. That had made learning to read very difficult, and preoccupied his elementary school teachers. There were so many tests to make The Invisible Boy see letters as letters. Their attempts always fell short. Letters always seemed to be more than just letters, and he couldn't un-see what He *actually* saw. "A" as an archway, "little" a bridge connecting two landforms comprised with "girl" and "named Goldilocks." The problem was, *only* The Invisible Boy could see these things. His teachers continued to test him and hope for the best.

When The Invisible Boy turned twelve he found a world to escape into. It was by accident. Another student named James had left a book in class. It was torn on the edges, well read, and well loved. It had rips, and stains. The pages had been turned over so many times the spine barely held the pages in. The Invisible Boy quickly grabbed the discarded book, a japanese novel, from the chair and tucked it in his backpack. He knew it was wrong to take something that wasn't his, but somehow The Invisible Boy felt compelled to take it. It was as if the image of two fighting warriors on the front cover, in deep blacks, and blue frozen in mid air, were beckoning him to follow. And, perhaps, they held the secret to learn how to survive the one place he wasn't invisible: The walk to and from his home to the bus stop.

Hector and Luis were the leaders of a gang of fifteen year-old teenage boys in his neighborhood in East Providence. The neighborhood gang of boys had dropped out of high school and sold drugs, partied hard, and threatened any boy in the neighborhood they desired. The Invisible Boy was a favorite target. *He* never fought back.

"Going to school amigo?" asked Hector.

"What a good boy," Luis replied.

"You might need this!" Hector said grabbing The Invisible Boy's backpack and throwing it to the gang of other boys to search for money.

While the other boys were busy destroying his backpack and tossing the contents onto the dirty cracked sidewalk, Hector pinned The Invisible Boy against the brick wall. Luis began to hit him in the stomach. The Invisible Boy's eyes looked for something to focus on to escape the pain. Today, he found something other than the sky—the japanese novel he had just taken on the ground. The Invisible Boy stared at the cover and concentrated on every tiny detail to try and block the pain. The warriors on the front gave him courage to take it like a warrior. He had been concentrating so hard, it had taken The Invisible Boy a moment to realize Hector and Luis had stopped and were now looking for a reaction. As if on cue, the Invisible Boy began to sob great tears. He knew the boys expected this. They wouldn't leave him alone until he showed them something.

"Aww, Hector, he's crying." Luis said, with a laugh.

And then they all left and headed down the opposite direction. This was the same every day. On the way home it might be rocks thrown at him, broken bottles, trash, or gum.

At home The Invisible Boy would retreat to the sanctuary of his bedroom. His mother and father worked late so The Invisible Boy would be home alone with his two little brothers. While his little brother's ate their snack and did their homework, The Invisible Boy would study his Japanese novel until it was time to make dinner. The Invisible Boy loved to trace the strange lines that made up each beautiful Japanese letter on the page. He soon began to understand the drawings on the page as if they were drawn from his own hand. *This* was the language He had been speaking fluently for years, *only* in his head. He would stay up all night in bed studying the images and tracing the lines with fingers, as his brothers slept in the bunk bed across from him. Every night he would escape into the stolen treasure. It was the only time The Invisible Boy felt happy. He smiled, and gave himself completely, mind, body, and soul to the world of anime.

There was only one downside to his newfound love—the issue of sleep. His nighttime rituals left him exhausted in school. During the day The Invisible Boy drifted between dreams of flipping the worn pages of the book at home and waking up to find himself back, in a classroom with his head down on a dirty table staring at the word "FUCK." Who knows how long he had slept? No one ever noticed though, he was invisible. His teachers were too busy trying to break up fights in the classroom, and managing the *very* visible students who didn't want to learn.

The Invisible Boy's quest into anime led him to steal a few other things from school, paper from the printer at the back of the room, some extra pencils off the teacher's desk. Things he hoped wouldn't be missed, but The Invisible Boy convinced himself *he* needed it more than they did. The Invisible Boy was now consumed with learning the art of drawing anime. His mother would *never* buy him a sketchbook. In his mother's world there were too many other things that money needed to be spent on. Instead of doing schoolwork he drew. His notebooks were tattooed and marked with anime. His artwork grew and spread like ink running on white paper. It grew like a field of wild flowers across a grassy field, popping up here and there.

First step in The Invisible Boy's drawing lessons were getting the hands and feet drawn correctly. They were the hardest parts of the human figure to draw correctly he surmised after many failed attempts. So, The Invisible Boy became an investigative reporter, a

great observer of the human feet and hands whenever he could. It was hard work, but The Invisible Boy felt compelled and driven to learn. The Invisible Artist examined his brother's toes when he washed the day's dirt of city living off them with a washcloth. The Invisible Artist watched the way his other brother would move his toy truck around the rug occasionally crushing a bug or a roach that happened to cross paths with plastic wheels. The Invisible Artist studied his own hands as they circled the dirty dishes with soap and water in the sink. The Invisible Artist even dared stare at his mother's hand holding a cigarette by the bars at the window. He got as far as the index finger when his mother would say, "¿Que te quiero?" Translation: *What do you want?*" The Invisible Artist knew better than to say even "nada" Translation: *nothing.*

But it wasn't "nothing." The Invisible Artist was hard at work learning to *be* an artist. Learning what it took to draw a warrior, to *be* a warrior. To draw one, you had to know what it felt like to be a warrior. Hands were important; feet were essential. Hands were weapons. They cut through the air to the opponent

like knives. Hands had to tell a story. The feet, a force on the page, that if drawn well, just might break through the page into an invisible world. Now, that The Invisible Artist had succeeded in imitation, it was time to create characters of his own. What a delight The Invisible Artist felt as his own hand and mind worked as one to create something new and something that was entirely his own. The Invisible Artist drew fight scenes between his main character Ley and The demon Shaki that felt like a slow film. Every line, every stroke, and The Invisible Artist felt what it must be like to have true happiness in the world. Success and accomplishment.

It is the year 2030, the world is feared being taken over by a demon named Shaki. Ley, a quiet high school student by day, warrior by night, is the only person strong and smart enough to take on the demon Shaki. Shaki had gotten his powers from a nuclear plant scientist Mr. Kanaki who created him to take over the world. But Shaki turned on his creator and killed him in a fierce battle.

One day, The Invisible Artist became visible again everywhere. That day he became his namesake again. Christian awoke early in the morning to the sounds of shouting from the people who lived in the apartment below. Christian's eyes followed the sun peeking through the homemade red curtains that framed the barred window. The point of the sunbeam landed in the center of his little brother Jose´'s thick black curly head of hair. Jose´ was sitting on the floor with one of Christian's sketchbooks in his hands. Jose´ carefully flipped through the pages tracing the images with his fingertips. Christian wanted to preserve this quiet moment forever in his mind. Christian lay as still as he could so as not to disturb Jose´. As if he sensed his brother's gaze Jose´ slowly turned around to look at his brother. The two brothers stared at each other. The look in Jose´'s eyes was amazement. Jose´ looked at Christian like he was a superhero. At that exact moment Christian became visible in the world. Christian felt happiness through Jose´'s eyes. Jose´ gave him gravity on the earth where He had only floated before.

"¿Puedes enseñgarme?" Translation: *Can you teach me?*

Jose´ was a great student. Jose´ was patient and attentive. He loved his "maestro". Translation: *teacher*. Jose´ liked learning how to draw. Christian wasn't sure when it happened, but Jose´ began adding words to the drawings. This time it was Jose´ who surprised Christian. Christian and Jose´ continued their weekend rituals of lessons. The joy and contentment that filled their Saturday mornings were pure bliss. Then a bomb exploded. It wasn't an actual bomb but the damage was as lethal. Christian was failing school and his mother exploded on him with the rage and fury of a real atomic bomb. Christian could do nothing but brace himself and take the punishment being served. Christian knew this day would arrive. Christian dropped out of school and started a job working with his father doing construction. When Christian came home exhausted from the physical labor and long hours, he remained awake long enough to look over Jose´'s latest creation.

Years flew by. Christian moved out of the apartment and Jose´ barely saw him. Christian worked double shifts at the construction site and couldn't come by to see his little brother anymore. So Jose´ would stop by his work and bring a snack for Christian. Jose´ would show Christian his latest creation. One of those visits, Christian gave Jose´ a flyer for a summer program called Youth AS220. It offered the chance to be an artist and get paid for it.

"This should be *you,* Christian," Jose´ said as he held the flyer in his hands.

"Too late for me, but not for you Jose´." Christian replied with a smile.

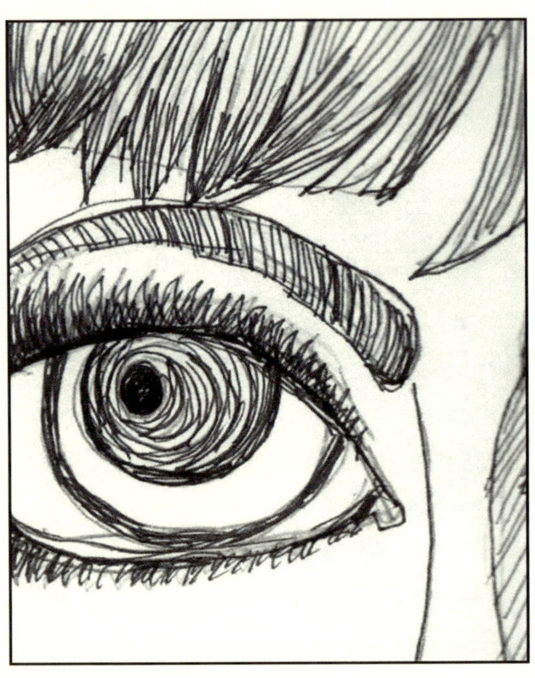

At Youth AS220 Jose´ got paid to make art, and he heard a young artist named Nick Shelby speak. That was a day that changed everything for Jose´. He saw the possibility. He saw hope. Nick was traveling the world and getting paid for his artwork. Nick came to speak to the kids about how he grew up and where he came from, and how it took a lot of hard work to get to where he had been, and a lot of help. He said, "*Never* be afraid to ask for help as an artist. You *always* need help, and there are people out there willing to give it. I would not be where I was without the help I got from people who believed in me."

Everyone he met at AS220 was like family. Jose´ felt the

community welcome him in. It felt good to make art, talk, write, and create in a place that felt safe. That summer Jose´ wrote and illustrated his first novel. It was only a small pamphlet on cheap copier paper, but it was *his* creation. He dedicated it to Christian. It was titled *Christian El Champión*. The Invisible Artist, Christian, was alive and well, fighting enemies of the world. When Jose´ got up at the Youth Studio event he proudly talked about his work, and Christian stood in the back smiling at his little brother and former student.

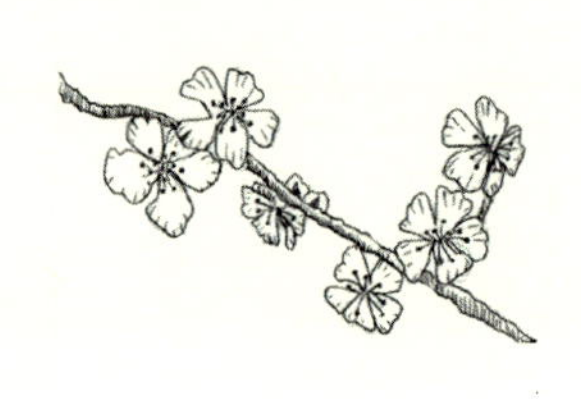

If You Can't Hack it Please Leave

Most of Hannah's first semester at RISD was spent studying the human form. Hannah's drawing teacher Ms. Liliana was what she had always imagined an artist should look like. She had long brown hair, dressed in jeans and tee shirts, and maybe a men's slouchy cardigan, when it got cold. Ms. Liliana was not classically beautiful but she was cool and hip, and spoke with her hands in the air. Hannah and her classmates spent hours at Ms. Liliana's beck and call. Ms. Liliana was so beguiling as a person, not only did she look like an artist; she had the essence of "artist." Ms. Lilliana would fluidly speak about lines, and segue seamlessly into to a story about doing a similar exercise as she sat on the bank of the Seine eating cheese and bread. Ms. Liliana had lived in so many amazing places, and Hannah could vividly see herself following in Ms. Liliana's footsteps as an artist...Paris, Barcelona, New York, and Florence to name only a few. This is what Hannah had imagined RISD would be like.

Hannah had always thought the hardest part about going to RISD was getting in, until she met Mr. McKinley in her 2D freshman foundation class. From the first class Mr. McKinley seemed to hone in on Hannah as someone he intensely disliked. Mr. McKinley was the polar opposite of Ms. Liliana. Mr. McKinley looked like he had just stepped off a yacht from Cape Cod. He was middle aged, with a protruding potbelly, grayish beard that offset a pair of bland boring brown eyes, and a face that looked he belonged at Harvard; not an art school like RISD.

In Mr. McKinley's 2D class everyone worked with gouache, a thick paint, which left marks of imperfection or streaks if done incorrectly. Hannah found it an incredibly stifling media and it filled her with rage at the pretentiousness of perfection it exacted. Hannah sat for hours trying to make monochromatic boxes of perfect even color and no streaks, and had to toss more than a few of the expensive boards. For Hannah, the worst part of classes at school was "the crit." The class hung up their assignment each week at the front board, all side by side for a comparison. Mr. McKinley would start innocuously enough discussing the point of the assignment just completed: *To learn about monochromatic color-gradations and shades.* But then Mr. McKinley's critique would begin to turn into a competition of who could tear down someone's piece the best. Mr. McKinley seemed to get a twinkle in his eye when he came to Hannah's piece. Mr. McKinley would gather the group up to inspect her assignment and shred it to bits. But more than shredding it to bits, the goal seemed to be to shred her as a person as well.

Hannah swore she would never cry in front of the class, but one day she did. Mr. McKinley hit her core when he said, "I'm

not sure if you are RISD material, and you will NEVER be a Nick Shelby!" Everyone had heard about his famous nephew once they came to RISD. Hannah began to believe Mr. McKinley. Maybe she *wasn't* cut out for RISD. Maybe she would *never* be an artist. When the semester came to a close Hannah found she had received an incomplete from Mr. McKinley's class. When she entered Mr. McKinley's office to discuss the matter, he was on the phone but waved her in anyway. Hannah sat in the very uncomfortable fake Herman-Miller-like chair. Hannah secretly cringed at Mr. McKinley's office—which was decorated with all knock offs and replicas of famous art pieces. On his desk a small version of *The Dancer* by Degas; On the walls prints of Monet's *Water Lillies Series*, and Picasso's *Guernica*. Hannah's thoughts began to wander freely as Mr. McKinley kept her waiting. *What kind of a person would collect these things? What does it say about how they feel about art is this world? People whom only go by the name brand but not the real thing?* It made her dislike him even more. Yet he held all the power. She shrunk in the chair waiting for him to address her.

When Mr. McKinley finally recognized her presence, Hannah tried her best to not let her dislike for him or her emotion over things he'd said get the best of her. She wanted in and out as fast as she could. Hannah rationalized as best as she could with Mr. McKinley, and had smartly brought her portfolio on hand as proof of her argument. After all that, she wound up with a C in his class, but at least she would *never* have to deal with him again. In this, was a small victory, at least now she could get down from the cross Mr. McKinley had hung her on. And it *did* feel like a small relief as she entered her second semester.

Her relief was short-lived. This time her problems were out of the classroom. Her roommate Elana had seemed all right in September. Elana was so busy and intent upon her social life they rarely saw

each other. All that changed, second semester, when Elena got a boyfriend name Skin. Skin was a hipster in the worst way. Skin was rich but dressed poor. He was a painter, but Hannah never saw him paint. In fact, he was one of the kids at RISD that she noticed didn't seem to do much work at all, but *never* seemed to get kicked out. Skin was at RISD for a good time. Elana and Skin liked to do cocaine together, and have sex so loud that everyone could hear them doing it, up and down the hallway. Hannah soon began carrying all her supplies and art projects with her all the time like a homeless person, and sleeping in her clothes in the dorm's main lounge.

One day, everything came to a head…

Hannah walked into the room and found Skin alone in Elana's bed passed out half naked in his boxers. Hannah had knocked loudly but no one answered. Hannah even turned the key loudly and pushed it open so it would slam against the wall before she actually placed her body in the room. Hannah saw Skin in bed and cringed, but he seemed out cold so she grabbed her remaining clothes and stuffed them into a bag, exploding with art supplies.

All of a sudden she felt a strong arm wrap itself around her skinny one and turn her around, "What the fuck are you doing in here stealing Elana's shit!!!"

Hannah turned around to face Skin's expansive chest and he was holding her arm so tight it felt like it was going to break. Hannah looked in Skin's eyes and his pupils were extremely large. *He must be on something, she thought.*

"Could you let go of my arm *please*? You're hurting me!" Hannah said shrinking into the pain that was beginning to make her feel like her arm might fall off.

Just then Elana walked in and started laughing. Hannah couldn't believe it. Elana thought this was funny. Skin finally let go and told her to, "Stay the fuck out of here!" "Here", i.e., meaning out of *her* room. And the door slammed in her face. *Her door. No longer.* Hannah stood there for quite a bit of time in shock. But then, it was as if something clicked in Hannah at that moment. It was a sink or swim moment. Hannah decided she *was* meant to be here at RISD. She *would* make it. She *would* make her own destiny and stop letting people get in the way of *her* destiny. Hannah told the RA what had been happening. Skin and Elana got kicked out of the dorm. Hannah gave Elana a special surprise too. Hannah had spray painted "I suck" on a very expensive white t-shirt of hers, while Elana and Skin had been with the RA. *Won't she be surprised when she unpacks,* thought Hannah. Hannah laid back on her bed and fell into a well deserved restful sleep for the first time in months.

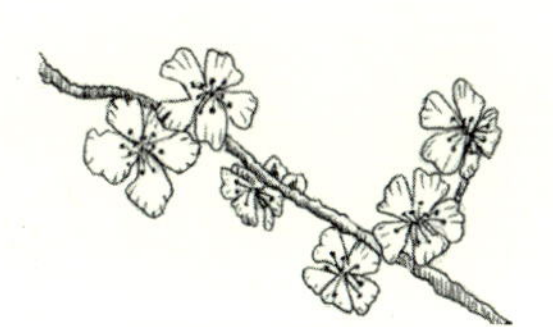

The Walking Gallery

Hank had seen people from every walk of life in his tattoo parlor. To Hank, tattoos, were like walking pieces of art. The world was his gallery. Hank had dedicated his life to his parlor and every inch of his store had something sentimental to him. The most sentimental item, was a bell from his great grandmother over the front door. The front door jingled every time a customer walked in. It was an oddly sweet sound for his profession and clientele, but Hank liked it that way. Hank liked *that* kind of irony. He never knew what that ringing bell would bring him each time. Hank had created tattoos for businessman, fraternity boys, punk rockers, soldiers, you name it—Hank had met them all.

Hank was a patient man and went about his job like a master artist. He could deal with people's indecisions as if they were merely stops in his work. When Hank was done with a tattoo there was always a sense of camaraderie between him and the person now wearing his artwork. Hank thought that art could do that to people. Bring people together in admiration and the pleasure of enjoying something visceral. Hank thought a lot about these things. We all have eyes, heart and a brain that reacts to beauty. And even if you *never* wanted to get a tattoo, there's something about body art that always does catch even the eye of a staunchly conservative businessman walking down the street. You *have* to look. That is what art does to people. And with the jingle of his great grandmother's bell Hank's art would never be viewed again by him unless by chance. Perhaps, that's what made the moment feel so exciting and special, and never to repeated in the same way again.

The whole process to Hank was ritualistic. First, Hank put on some gloves, took out a bottle of rubbing alcohol, and delicately cleansed the area of his human canvas with a couple white fluffy cotton balls. Next, he took a ballpoint pen and began to draw the image the customer had chosen. Glancing occasionally at the tattoo book in front of him for reference about a particular detail. Hank was an amazing artist, just as careful and delicate about the body art as Picasso was to a painting. As the image emerged each time, Hank felt the joy of the process of creation. He forgot space and time and location.

Next, Hank pulled out the fresh needles from their sterile packages. The *whirr* of the machine would commence as Hank began to insert the first ink into the skin. Hank had the hands of a surgeon when the needles were in his hands. The expertise and precision that Hank had with the contact of the tip of the needle to the skin was something to be seen. It kept many people from passing out. After Hank finished he dabbed on a huge swab of thick petroleum jelly to prevent bleeding, protect the ink, and allow the ink to set in. Last, Hank and the customer would admire the final piece in mutual satisfaction. Out of nowhere it seemed, as like Rodin imagined rock into sculpture, the art would appear as if it had been hidden there all the time inside the person's skin.

Hank had recently hired a young boy named Nick Shelby to work his front desk. Since Nick had started working there, the place seemed even more like home. Hank couldn't put his finger on it, but he saw great things happening from this boy, if only he had someone to help guide him. Hank felt the satisfaction that he had at least kept Nick from running the street with the pack of boys that were always up to no good.

Hank had a business partner who was a childhood friend named Charlie. As young kids Hank and Charlie had dreamed together about opening a tattoo shop, and both determined, had seen it through. However, the path to the tattoo shop was not a straight one. Their paths had taken many turns away from each other. His friend Charlie had gone to college and a Masters in Business. While, Hank had fallen in love with a girl in the neighborhood, and worked odd jobs, and did tattooing on the side.

In the beginning, Hank ran his tattoo shop out of their apartment. Hank was happy enough with making enough to make ends meet, and then Charlie's path merged with Hank's again. Charlie had bought some buildings in downtown Providence and offered a storefront to Hank. Charlie made Hank a great offer, in fact, it was so fluid Hank didn't think twice. Hank had always taken the path of least resistance. Charlie gave Hank the space in return for a small percentage of Hank's business.

In a short amount of time, Hank was doing so well in his new home that he always gave Charlie more than a small percentage. Perhaps, that's what set off the change in Charlie. After a year, Charlie soon began to see dollar signs instead of his friend. The day Charlie's new trait had exhibited itself to Hank, Charlie had shown up without his usual advance notice. Hank was curious. They had already had their business day to trade money, their morning coffee together, and Charlie was usually busy with all of his buildings the rest of the week. So Hank was baffled as to the reason Charlie would show up on this extra day. His first response was concern, but Hank focused on finishing his task at hand, the mail worker receiving a tattoo.

"Charlie, I'll be with you in a second," said Hank as he gently rubbed on a large swath of petroleum jelly over an intricate Chinese dragon in a fighting position, with a spine of red and black patterns, on the shoulder of the extremely large man. Even with Charlie waiting, Hank paused to admire the work with his customer. There was a moment of calm silence between the two men in appreciation of the final piece, which shone under the coat of petroleum jelly that protected it. Nick walked over silently and also stood in admiration. Then Hank and the man shook hands.

"Nick, you can ring him up." Hank said.

Hank smiled as he watched Nick talking to the man about his tattoo as he worked the cash register. Then Hank walked to the back office, which also served as a small storage closet filled with supplies from floor to ceiling. Hank found Charlie sitting in one of two fold out chairs. The room was separated from the main space with curtains that Hank's girlfriend Minnie had sewn. The curtains were covered in a pattern of cars from the 1940s—Desotos, Packards, and Fords in a matte color palette of sea foam green, deep reds, and black. An era Hank very much admired stylistically. The lines, the angles, and the colors, were forever classic in Hank's mind. In the center of the very small room, there was a small wooden fold out table where Hank would eat lunch. Other than the curtains, the room was quite spare and utilitarian, much like Hank. Hank took the seat across from Charlie. He waited silently for Charlie to speak.

"So Hank, I've been thinking. You have been doing really well business wise. In fact, I am quite impressed that word of mouth could do such business. It goes against every model I ever studied in college." Charlie said with a careful laugh. "Anyway, I was thinking if we did a few things, business cards, some ads online, mail chimp, you know we could raise our prices and you and I could be sitting pretty."

Hank pondered the words in silence. Charlie was used to this odd quirk characteristic of his childhood friend, and waited as patiently as he could.

After a minute Hank simply replied, "Why?"

"Well...you could definitely retire earlier." Charlie said with a smile that looked contrived.

"I'm not going to retire Charlie. *This* is my life." Hank replied with a smile that was genuine and honest.

"Yeah, I *know* Hank." Charlie said looking a bit defeated in his body posture, the businessman in him sinking away into the concrete floor below.

There was a moment of brief silence on the part of both of them, but only Hank seemed to really embrace it.

"If you had more money you could do some traveling, hire some other people to run the shop. Take a vacation?" Charlie continued, now sounding desperate.

"I fish every Monday." Hank replied, and continued seamlessly. "Do you want me to pay you more Charlie?"

"Well, no." Charlie said and stopped.

"I don't mind. I have plenty especially when the nice folks in here leave me tips. I could share that with you as well." Hank replied and then looked concerned, "Are you okay Charlie? You aren't in trouble, are you?"

Charlie looked completely defeated and shook his head to gesture the answer was 'no.'

"I have to go. I will see you at our regular time. Just forget about all this. It was a *stupid* idea." Charlie said looking at his phone and then heading out through the curtains.

"I hope you find what you are looking for Charlie. I wonder sometimes." Hank said to himself, as Charlie was long gone.

Hank sat in silence with his eyes closed for several minutes. When he opened them the blue eyes of Nick twinkled before him.

Nick knew better than to interrupt Hank in his state of quiet. Nick had grown accustomed to his boss sitting silently, and he respected it—*even* admired it. Nick waited for Hank to speak.

"There are people who will look at your talent and just see dollar signs. You can't avoid them in life." Hank said and paused in more silent thought. "People want to better the world and some people want to better their wallet." The bell jingled, and he said, "Nick, tell my new customer I will be right with him."

Hank walked to his work area and Nick led a young teen-

age boy with a piercing in his nose, cheeks, and tongue over to Hank. The boy held out a scrawled drawing on lined notebook paper for Hank to inspect. Hank looked at the paper and stood quietly. The teenage boy shifted his hands into the deep pockets of his black pants. The boy scratched his jet-black hair and crossed his arms over the chest of his t-shirt that spelled out "Punk Rock Or Die." The boy pursed his thin lips and waited for a reply from Hank. Nick was used to this, but the teenage boy looked like he was going to literally die if Hank didn't say something soon.

Nick was about to give the boy a look of understanding when Hank finally replied, "Might I show you something that you won't tire of?" Hank's smile was so honest that no customer took offense when Hank posed questions like these. The teenage boy shrugged a reluctant 'yes'. Hank continued, "Let's see…Nick, hand me the blue binder." Nick reached up to the shelf behind the counter and handed it to Hank, and then Hank did what he was so good at—help guide people through a decision that would last the rest of their life. Soon the boy was smiling like a little kid and in the barber chair getting a tattoo of a Bengal Tiger running in a most noble position, mid air ready to catch something.

After the boy paid and left it was quiet and Hank enjoyed some fresh air while Nick manned the phones and booked appointments. Hank walked back in after five minutes escorting a very attractive girl with red, blonde, and white striped hair that brought out her green catlike eyes. She had an air of confidence that seemed to stare right through Nick.

"Do you need to look at the books?" Nick asked.

"Nope," she replied, "Got a picture right here." She placed a printout of a graphic rose image from the 1920s. "Like?"

"Sweet." Nick replied. "I like 1920s art too."

"Cool. I'm Gretchen." She said with a smile showing her perfectly straight white teeth.

"Nick." He said.

Hank waved Gretchen over and she glided over to the barber chair in her washed out blue jeans that were shredded from wear. They talked for a while and Hank drew the ballpoint image onto the inside of her wrist. Hank looked down at the young girl and noticed how thin she seemed.

"You eaten today?" Hank asked with fatherly concern.

"Oh, yeah. I'm fine." Gretchen replied quickly.

"Well, it's almost dinner time for us, I'll get you something just in case." Hank said. "Don't want you passing out on me."

"Nick, order us some dinner, and something extra for Gretchen here. She says she's eaten, but if she did it wasn't a lot. I know these things right, Nick?" He held up a twenty and a ten in his hand and laughed.

"He does." Nick said to Gretchen. "Any requests."

"Salad." Gretchen said.

"Get that Chicken Parm sub for me, and some extra bread for this girl." Hank said.

When Hank was done with Gretchen's tattoo the food arrived.

Nick came over to check out the final tattoo on Gretchen's wrist. It was lovely, and Hank had matched the original drawing with precision and expertise.

Gretchen showed her pearly whites, "Beautiful, Hank. Just, exquisite. You *are* the finest artist I've ever met."

She paid up and tried to give Hank money for the food. Hank just shook his head. "On me kid. You, *need* to eat."

"But my tattoo only cost thirty bucks? That would mean you made almost nothing off me?" Gretchen asked looking confused.

"Well, sometimes, Gretchen, *other* things are more important than money. You'll understand when you are an adult." Hank replied.

Before Gretchen could reply Hank continued, "Let's eat."

Gretchen followed Nick and Hank into the back storeroom/office, and Nick stood so that Gretchen could have one of the two chairs. They sat in silence for a while. Gretchen picked at her salad while Hank and Nick ate hungrily.

"You in high school too?" Gretchen asked Nick.

"Yep. Tenth Grade. You?" Nick asked Gretchen.

"The same." Gretchen replied. A text message bleeped on her phone. "I have to run. Thanks guys. *Really.*"

Hank listened and watched the two teenagers with a smile on his face.

"You barely touched your salad Gretchen. You sure you feel all right to leave?" Hank asked.

To an outsider it would have looked like a strange family meeting, but it *wasn't* a meeting at all, and it *wasn't* family.

"I'll unlock the door for you." Nick said and walked out of the storeroom followed by Gretchen.

"Oh wait, I almost forgot Gretchen. Let me take a picture for the wall. Yours is a nice one. It needs to don the wall." Hank said wiping the red sauce off his beard.

Gretchen posed showing the inside of her wrist. Hank walked back inside and looked at the picture on his phone. Hank felt content and happy with his art for the day. He began to go about carefully arranging his tools and making sure the inks were stored properly. Hank's happiness was short lived when Nick burst back into the store, the bell ringing wildly from the force of the opening. Nick shouted, "Hank! Help! Gretchen! She's passed out! Call 911! She just fell onto the sidewalk!"

Within a few minutes the ambulance came and took Gretchen away. Hank locked up the store and Nick and him got into Hank's truck and headed to the hospital.

"You think she'll be all right Hank?" Nick asked looking worried.

"Yes. Seen it before." Hank replied without explaining.

They drove in silence, and Hank finished, "She just needs to eat. Beautiful girl…doesn't think she is skinny enough, not realizing she might disappear forever if she keeps getting thinner and thinner."

Hank shook his head. Then turned to Nick, "She'll be just fine kid. *Trust* me."

And Nick did trust Hank. Hank was the only trustworthy person he had ever known in his fifteen years on this earth.

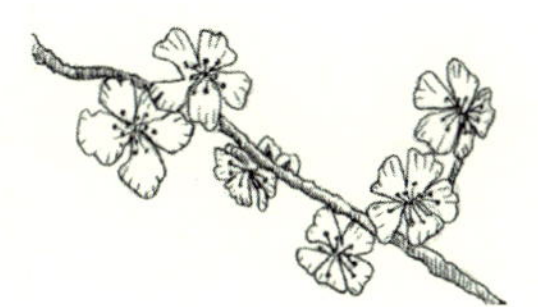

A Lightness of Being

Amelia, a six year old girl, sat cross-legged in purple shorts and multi-colored shirt. Amelia's mother Jane sat a few feet away from her daughter on the steps of the wooden porch of the three-decker apartment building they lived in. The street they lived on was lined with similar rental buildings with vinyl siding and rickety wooden stairs that had been painted over so many times the sides were rough and bumpy. The sidewalks were thin, cracked and bubbled up at points where the roots of old trees had broken through under the ground. A driveway wrapped around the side of each building for cars to park in the backyard. Since there was no proper back-yard (because of the parking area) Amelia always played out front in the few feet of driveway not taken up by cars. On any other day except Sunday there would be a plethora of kids out riding bikes and playing games on the street. Amelia was still too little to join in but she loved watching the kids play. However, today was Sunday, and while this was a poor neighborhood, it was extremely religious. Once the sun got higher, Jane and Amelia would watch the families pouring out of their apartments in their Sunday best for church—satin blue dresses, shiny mary janes, miniature pin stripe suits, and hats with flowers.

Jane watched her daughter drawing away to her heart's content, and felt a pang of envy. Jane remembered feeling that sense of bliss she saw in her daughter's face—before the weight of life, bills, and work had pulled her away from that sense of freedom. Last year, Jane had lost her job waitressing at *Heminways*. Jane had worked there for five years, and ever since then she balanced three jobs at different restaurants. Jane was a great waitress and she got good tips, it's just that times were tough for everyone and people gave as much as they could. Everyone that is, except the rich college kids in town who came in drunk and would forget to leave her a tip. Jane felt annoyed at the lack of respect those kids had for the classes below them. They would never know what it was like to struggle. At least Jane's landlord was very understanding whenever Jane was late on rent. He knew how hard life had treated her, and he watched over Jane and Amelia like a father.

Jane had adopted a spotted rescue dog named Molly who had brown eyes that twinkled— about the time her husband had walked out on them both. Amelia and the mess of a street dog had immediately taken to each other. Jane supposed there was an understanding between the two fatherless creatures in the world bound together by unconditional love. While Jane did most of the feeding, walking, and grooming, it was Amelia's bed that Molly went to every night. Jane's husband had left them after Amelia's third birthday to live with another woman named Kate. Kate was ten years younger and worked at his office. They had met an office party.

Jane never worked on Sundays even though they could have used the money. Jane wasn't sure why she had chosen Sunday. Perhaps because it was a Sunday when her husband had left. Sundays Jane paused from her busy life to mourn the loss and try and rehabilitate herself. It wasn't easy, but Jane had had enough experiences with men leaving her, that she could remind herself everything passed with time, and with a daughter that needed her she had no time to feel sorry for herself. Amelia was her healer.

This Sunday, like every Sunday, Amelia's face had the look of deep concentration. Her small pink mouth was smudged with dried peanut butter and jelly from the sandwich her mother left by her side on a pink plastic plate. Breakfast in the summer meant anything. Today, Amelia had asked for lunch for breakfast. Two yellow jackets were busy investigating Amelia's half eaten sandwich. Normally, the sight of bees sent Amelia into a teary screaming fit, but at the moment she was completely unaware of the bees close proximity. Amelia was immersed in her chalk drawing of a princess and knight riding on horseback, pushing back her pool streaked hair and bangs with her chalk stained hands when they got in the way of her view.

Amelia's mother walked over to admire her daughter's hard work on the pavement. Jane gave Amelia a kiss on the top of her head and a word of encouragement and then walked back over to the porch. Amelia loved drawing, and there was a calm unspoken peace that settled in on the driveway between mother and daughter. Amelia was as happy as a clam. If it had been the school year, and not summer, Jane would have never let Amelia get away with wearing her favorite clothes so many days in a row. Jane's daughter had tried to perfect the art of shower aversion but only in summer did it last more than a day. In the summer Jane was more willing to break the strict rules of fall, winter and spring.

"Mommy stand still. I'm going to draw you!" Amelia declared holding her chalk up in the air as if it was the exclamation point at the end of her sentence.

Amelia looked up at her mom and took a moment to study her mother. Amelia squinted and looked serious.

"Mommy, pretend I am a famous artist. *You* are my model. Now be still Mommy." Amelia ordered as she smudged green chalk across her face.

"Like this." Jane replied freezing into an awkward position.

"No silly Mommy! Natural. You can still drink your coffee. I can still draw you with little movements." Amelia replied with a giggle.

Jane smiled and picked up her coffee and newspaper. The color of the chalk gave way in gritty chunks that rained down and lay in a small pile of colorful dust on the surface of the hot concrete. Amelia focused on the thick piece of chalk in her hand as it touched the dark grey rough surface of the driveway below her. Occasionally a neighbor of theirs, Raina, would join them on a Sunday. When Raina showed up Amelia always gave her a royal welcome only a six year old could do —and it was always the same, filled with hugs and excitement. Today was no exception when Raina made an appearance.

"Hey Jane! Hi Amelia! Man, it's *too* hot to sleep!" Raina said wiping sweat off her forehead as she sat down on the porch next to Jane.

"Raina!!!!!!!!!" Amelia squealed and ran over to give Raina a hug, her chalk hands leaving small handprints on both sides of Raina's yellow summer dress.

"Amelia! You've got chalk on Raina's dress." Jane said looking embarrassed.

Raina smiled and said, "That color of chalk matches my dress so perfectly. You have the talent to be a fashion designer some day." Amelia giggled and looked up at Raina in awe. "What great drawings Amelia!" Raina continued enthusiastically which sent Amelia into a happy dance of hopscotch moves. Amelia took Raina's hand and squeezed it tightly. Then Amelia dragged Raina on a tour of her driveway drawings, and suddenly dropped down one point saying, "I've almost forgot! Molly in her flying motorcycle!"

It was a wonderful thing for Jane to watch her daughter be so in the moment. Try as she might, Jane couldn't remember the last time she had felt that way. Maybe, when she had fallen in love with Amelia's father.

Raina sat down next to Jane.

"Raina, want a cup?" Jane asked.

"Sure. Thanks Jane." Raina replied.

Jane returned a few minutes later with a cup for Raina. They sat side by side in silence sipping at their mugs of coffee and watching Amelia draw away to her hearts content.

"Wow. Wish I could be her for just an hour." Raina whispered quietly.

Jane and Raina stared at the little girl as she concentrated on each stroke and color she chose.

"I wish I could be that free." Raina said dreamily.

"Me too." Jane said to Raina with a sigh.

"Life just gets complicated sometimes, huh?" Raina said.

"You can say that a million times over." Jane replied with a sigh.

"Do you mind me asking Jane, how old was Amelia when her father left her?" Raina asked.

Jane was silent for a moment. Raina's question had caught her off guard. She hadn't been expecting that this morning. And on a Sunday, the day to work on her loss, not dwell.

"I'm sorry, Jane. I don't mean to intrude. Just, Amelia is such a happy little girl. You've done an amazing job. My father left when I was about Amelia's age and I was a blubbering mess. Actually my mother and I both were, for years. And well, it just seems like you've done an amazing job. Both of you seem so close and happy. When my father left, my mother blamed me and well at that moment I learned to shut the world out. I just focused on me, and surviving my mother's accusations until I was old enough to be free of it." Raina finished.

"No, it's not an intrusion, by you, at least. I'm sorry about your parents. That's awful. As far as Amelia and I go, I guess, call it survival too. You get the cards your dealt. Didn't plan to raise her myself but you know she's an amazing kid. All I've got to give her is love. I figure, that's free, so I give it as much as you can." Jane replied.

"Well, Amelia is the luckiest little girl I know. Wish I had an amazing mother like you. I might have not had this lingering feeling of always thinking something better is out there. It makes it hard for me to stay still. I'm not making much sense I'm sure. Amelia is lucky is all," Raina finished.

"Well, thank you." Jane said, "I think so too."

Raina and Jane sat drinking coffee in silence each focusing on Amelia in motion. They both seemed lost in their own deep thoughts, but yet simultaneously fixed on the motion of the chalk to the pavement guided by the imagination of the little six year old. The driveway was alive with color, lines, and movement. A few families on their way to church began to appear. As they passed Amelia, they stopped to admire the colorful space amidst the very commonplace street. It was impossible for anyone who passed to not pause and to enjoy Amelia's creations. They were, after all, so joyful and bright! Around eleven am Raina was off to work.

Jane got up to take a snapshot of Amelia's drawings on her phone. Jane had been doing that for three years now. Then Amelia and Jane would walk to the store to have prints made to hang up in Amelia's rom. In three years, Amelia's Sunday creations had covered one whole wall in her bedroom. It was her gallery. When Jane would put Amelia to bed, Amelia would tell her mother stories about how she had come up with each one. In this way, they could relive each Sunday together again. In these moments, it was her daughter Amelia that helped Jane remember, like all artists do, to live in the moment.

Jane's mother would babysit for Amelia when Jane had to work. If it hadn't been for Jane's mother, Jane and Amelia would have been out on the street. One night Jane's life turned upside down in a way she never quite expected, and unlike her husband's exit it was filled with something magical—a lightness of being you could say. That night began with her participating in a photo shoot for an online review of the restaurant she was working at. Jane happened to be the oldest waitress at the restaurant, but the photographer remarked, "the prettiest waitress" and had asked if Jane could pose for some of the pictures. Then Jane received an extremely large tip from a businessman who had dined alone. When Jane asked him if it was a mistake, the patron simply replied, "No. It's not a mistake. My wife just left me, and you were *so* nice. And the food was great. I needed this. Thanks." Jane served the filmmaker Wes Anderson and his crew, and then her upstairs neighbor Raina had appeared with a group of friends. Raina pulled Jane aside and handed her an invite to a late night party for the legendary fashion designer James Nicolar. "He's at the table." Raina said excitedly pointing out who he was. Jane laughed and said, "Thanks Raina."

At one a.m., Jane was exhausted but ecstatic about the amount of tips she'd made that night. Jane sat down at the bar and had a glass of white wine. As Jane finished up she dug for her keys out of her purse and out dropped the invitation from Raina along with two red lollipops, and a pink lipstick case. Jane placed the lipstick and lollipops away in her purse and then glanced at the invitation as she sipped her wine slowly. Jane admired the card of beautiful clothes that she could never afford and then placed the invitation down on the bar.

"Oh, you are going to that too?" said a patron sitting at the bar next to her.

Jane smiled at him and laughed, "No, I have a kid. I have to go home. I'm exhausted."

"You have a kid, how old are you?" The man asked nicely with a smile.

Jane noticed he wasn't bad looking.

"Yep. And it's time to relieve the babysitter." Jane said as she grabbed her keys and the invite and put it back in her purse—thinking Amelia loved looking at pretty things. This one would definitely be a card she would enjoy looking at.

"That's one lucky kid." The man said.

Jane laughed as she walked out of the restaurant to the back parking lot. She got in her car and started it up. Jane glanced in the rearview mirror and paused to look at her reflection and thought about the patron in the bar. *Well, not looking too shabby, Jane. Maybe you still have something.* She took out the invite and thought: *This has been the strangest night, what the hell!* She texted her mother: *be a little late, okay with u?* Her phone beeped back: *yes.* Jane paused for a moment, looked in the mirror and before she could change her mind reapplied some lipstick checked her hair and put the car in gear.

When Jane arrived at the party Raina waved her over and handed her a cosmopolitan in a pink and red plastic glass. Raina sat with Jane on a paisley couch and she brought a few people over to meet Jane. Mitchell was an author of Gothic Fiction; Ren

was a model, and Harry was a Professor. It was quite the eclectic mix. Jane wasn't sure if it was work, her age, or the cosmopolitan in her but she found it hard to keep track of who was who. Jane admired the ease at which Raina moved about the room. Everyone seemed drawn to Raina. Jane felt suddenly old, lonely, and tired and was beginning to regret her decision to come. Jane put her drink down on the coffee table (a log of wood split in half with a piece of glass resting on top of it). She was beginning to feel like a five-dollar dress that had been hung on the most expensive rack of clothing.

"You're not leaving *already?*" It was James Nicolar and he sat down with elegance and grace next to Jane on the couch and continued with a light laughter in his voice, "It is *my* party after all, and we haven't had the pleasure of speaking, have we? Monsieur Nicolar at your service, and you are?"

"Jane. Raina invited me." She said with a smile. James Nicolar had an air of sophistication and grace, quite missing, Jane thought, from the present generation of men. It made her smile, and she didn't quite know why.

"Ah, Raina. L'enfant." James said, "Lovely girl, but so, I don't know…*undirected?*"

"Yes, she is quite lovely. Both inside and out." Jane replied lifting her glass back up to take another sip of the sweet drink. Now, that James had joined Jane on the couch she didn't feel quite so ready to leave. After all a fashion designer was now looking at her, even if she felt like the five-dollar dress. James was so intriguing and as far from the world Jane revolved in. *He* was an artist. *She* was working class. The two just normally didn't meet. Jane knew he was a famous fashion designer, but he seemed so different than she had imagined a fashion designer would be. He was certainly dressed like one would imagine a famous fashion designer would dress: in black slacks, a button down shirt, a velvet smoking jacket, a flower ascot around his neck, thick black glasses, and a wonderful Charlie Chaplin hat that sat over his white head of well groomed hair. However, he did not seem to have the air of desperation and attention seeking she'd seen so many times on those runway carpets for the Oscars, or those fashion shows on late night television. James Nicolar seemed more like a director watching his play of a party unfold around him.

"Raina. Well, she *could* have it all." James Nicolar continued. "But she has no…well, no drive. She flits around from one thing to the next like a butterfly seeking nectar from every flower. But you see, she never stops fluttering long enough to decide what kind of a butterfly she wants to be? I have tried. Even hired her once. Was a *complete* disaster, No commitment."

Jane was confused, and her drink was getting to her head, but she was very much enjoying James's company. Jane had never experienced this kind of a conversation with a man. It was *so* nice, and James was so easy to talk to.

"*Ahhh,* I have a daughter like that, named Amelia. She never stops." Jane said with a laugh. "She is such a happy little girl though. To be that young again and without responsibilities."

"We do always have that lingering feeling, the older we get, but we don't have to lose it completely. I find that there is sense of power, also, the older we get. We have experience, and we have knowledge that these little butterflies lack." James Nicolar said with a smile and elegantly took a sip of his drink.

"Cheers to that James." Jane said, and they clinked glasses.

"My darling, *you* are a lovely woman. Do you mind if I do a little something to show you? A little of my touch?" James asked.

"Sure. Why not?" Jane laughed.

James took Jane's hair down and styled it with his hands. He took off his flower ascot and tied it like a headband in Jane's hair.

"Do you have some makeup in your purse?" James asked.

Jane handed him some eyeliner, mascara, and lipstick. He worked on Jane quickly and with a gentle touch. He was an artist concentrating on his work, which at the moment just so happened to be her. Jane began to feel a sense of lightness come across her being. She felt young. She felt beautiful. She felt *wonderful!* She felt like a piece of art.

"Ahh. You look like one of my models, Cherie, I used to work with in New York." James said with a smile.

Jane laughed and said, "Thank you."

James said, "Now, go on and go look in the bathroom mirror. You must appreciate it, it won't last forever, this makeup. Nothing good ever does. However, Madame, you may keep the ascot. It looks much nicer on you and I have a million more at home."

Jane went to the bathroom and looked in the mirror. She looked as lovely as she felt. She headed out determine to thank James Nicolar, but he had disappeared again. The party had also grown in size. She could barely move to look and see if she could find where James had gone. Raina found her first, and pulled her through the crowd to a small space where people where dancing. Jane felt the room slow down to the beat of the music. Jane was a bit woozy from the drink and the sensation of the music, crowd of people, and darkness of the room transported her. Jane felt young, wild and free. Jane felt like she was floating in space.

Then like Cinderella, midnight for Jane had long since struck and she quietly exited the party and somehow managed to catch a cab, where there never was one. Just a lucky night, Jane guessed—A magical night. Jane unlocked the door to her apartment as quietly as she could, slipped out her heels, and put her purse and keys on the table. Jane found her mother asleep on the couch, and she pulled a blanket over her. Then, Jane slid into her bed fully dressed and passed out.

The next morning Amelia bounced on the bed and drowned Jane with kisses. "I love you mommy. You look so beautiful today. Did a magical fairy do your hair and makeup last night while I slept?"

Jane thought of James Nicolar, and replied, "Yes. The magical fairy made mommy feel beautiful. How about some chocolate chip pancakes this morning?"

In the kitchen Jane blasted music and danced with Amelia as she made pancakes. Jane felt renewed. Jane even sat on the pavement out front and drew pictures with her daughter. She felt like a little girl, free wild, and wonderfully reborn. She knew it wouldn't last forever, but just like James Nicolar had reminded her, she was going to enjoy it while she could.

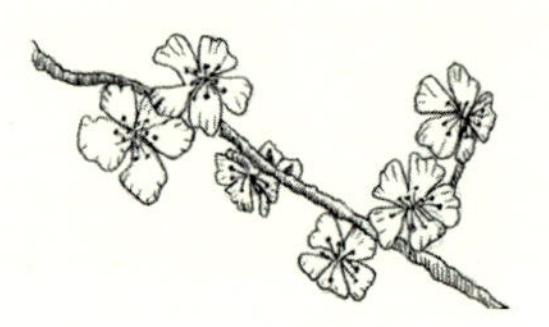

Go Ask Alice If It Was a Dream

Halloween was the biggest holiday celebrated at RISD. It went the whole week. Students spent all week preparing costumes, accessories, plans, and parties. You could go from one end of the East side to the other the week of Halloween and still not make it to all the parties that were happening. Charlotte, originally from Iowa, was a printmaking major. Charlotte had grown up on a farm and was used to heavy machinery like tractors, that's why she loved printmaking. All those machines with their process and procedures, felt completely natural to a farm girl like Charlotte. Lily, from Georgia, was a jewelry major. Charlotte and Lily were making their preparations in their dorm. Their friend Doug had gotten a bag of mushrooms, and the three of them went thriftshopping to find some costumes. Lily and Charlotte found roller skates to dress as roller derby girls. Doug found a short curly blonde wig and a garish puffy sleeved shiny pink gown to be a drag queen.

"Oh come on Doug! That's not a costume for you! That's your future profession!" Charlotte said playfully acknowledging Doug's well-known secret of his desire to dress like a woman as much as he could in this life.

"I can't help it! It's the only thing that 'called to me' in this drab store of boring clothes!" Doug said gesturing with his hands in the air. "But you ladies are being inventive! Like *very* much!"

Doug was a fashion major and he could create the most amazing clothes out of next-to-nothing. He was always fixing Charlotte and Lily's clothes into something new and wonderful. In return they took turns cooking dinner for Doug. It could be said it was a friendship of convenience, but they were really fond of their time spent together.

The party of the night was being thrown by a senior film major Justin, infamous for throwing parties that turned into his art projects for school. The parties were staged and people given scripts at the door along with alcohol and an assortment of drugs spread around in candy dishes. This was to assist the actors to "become" their part. All three of them had been to a few of his parties and it was never a let down. The creativity and suspense of the entire evening was quite a thrill.

Lily and Charlotte decided to skate over to Doug's that evening. Doug only lived a few blocks away, but he had insisted he was not walking in high heels from their apartment just to "get dressed" and have a before party. The mushrooms were streaming through Charlotte and Lily half way to their destination, and

their neon ankle straps were leaving a trail of rainbow colors in the air. They rolled over fields of fallen orange and yellow leaves, and passed rows of silent wooden houses that lined the streets. The houses seemed to stretch and shrink in size as if they were breathing. The old oak trees cast long shadows that bent crookedly up and down the sidewalk in a zigzag pattern.

"Check it out!!!" Charlotte said as she circled in loops.

"So amazing." Lily said following her lead.

"I feel like a cartoon!" Charlotte shouted and whistled loudly.

Charlotte and Lily found it hard not to laugh with the mushrooms turning the world around them into a funhouse with colors bright and dreamlike. Streetlights were small planets orbiting around them. Signs with letters rearranged magically from sense to nonsense and back again. The letters on the Stop sign became Pots and then Stop again.

Lily and Charlotte followed each other until they rolled right into a cop, or someone in costume of a cop. Halloween plus mushrooms meant sorting the truth difficult.

"Where are you going ladies?" the guy dressed as a cop smiled at them.

Lily and Charlotte couldn't help but keep cracking up.

"Nice costumes." The cop said, "Don't exceed the speed limit."

"Good one." Lily said sarcastically as Charlotte dragged her on.

They continued to roll on the streets of Providence enjoying the spiral world of dizzying colors. Rainbows of beautiful colors cycled around them, and everything from the lampposts to street signs were bending neon hues quite like looking through a prism. The world was like a soundtrack from a film: timeless, beautiful, and slow. As they increased their speed, Charlotte lifted her face to the sky to inhale the wind. Lily was looking down as her feet moved as if they were disconnected from her own body. They were lost in their timeless space, what seemed like an eternity. And then the real world called them back down from outer space.

"Hey Charlotte and Lily!" Charlotte was the first to look toward the sound of the voice eminating out of a large oak tree.

Lily spun around almost slamming into Charlotte saying, "What was that?"

"You don't recognize me Charlotte?" The voice came out into the air.

It seemed to vibrate in Charlotte's ears. As her eyes adjusted she finally made out a vampire and a Frankenstein shadow of figures next to the grand tree. It was Charlotte's crush, Ben. Charlotte had met Ben in her Drawing class and had been lusting after him for months. Charlotte grabbed Lily who was had been distracted again by something flashing before her eyes, and skated in a zigzag over to the guys on the sidewalk as Lily trailed her like she was on an amusement ride.

Charlotte wavered as she listed on the uneven pavement trying to will her body to stop moving. Lily's pupils were like canon balls and she sat down on the sidewalk and began spinning the wheels of her roller-skates.

"Holy shit Ben! No." Charlotte smiled and swayed on her wheels.

"Where you headed?" Ben asked.

"We are going to Justin's party." Charlotte replied. In her mind she was still and cool in front of the guy she had crushed on for so long. In reality she was rolling side to side.

"Party got busted by the cops just now. That's where we were coming from." Frankenstein answered. "Didn't recognize me either huh? Lane?"

Suddenly Lily looked up from her spinning wheel and replied, "Lane, hey."

Lily worked at the coffee shop with him. He had the most amazing blue eyes. Lily hadn't thought twice about Lane but in her present state she felt magnetized to Lane. The night seemed to have a magical quality to it. Like they were in a movie, and the script had been written specifically for these events to happen in the sequence they were occurring.

"I think we just ran into the cop that busted the party. He looked pretty happy. Your eyes are sooooooo blue." Lily smiled. Lane's eyes looked like they were glowing in the dark night.

"Party is moving to the tunnel want to come?" Lane asked.

So, all four headed for the tunnel. Lily and Lane following behind Charlotte and Ben. As they passed by a small park, Lily was distracted by a garden of flowers that seemed to be vibrating neon yellow colors in the dark. "You see that! *Woah!*"

Lily dragged Lane with her. Charlotte and Ben followed, but Ben stopped a little behind the other two and pulled Charlotte towards him and started kissing her. Charlotte lost sight of Lily, and soon she was rolling in the grass with Ben making out with him. The world was spinning and it was just Charlotte and Ben,

Ben and Charlotte. It was a wonderful delirious feeling. Then Ben said something, but Charlotte couldn't make it out. Ben said, "Are you okay? What are you on Charlotte?"

"Mushroooooooooms. "Charlotte tried to get the word out but her mouth felt like jelly.

"Nice. I did an amazing painting on mushrooms." Ben said and leaned down to kiss Charlotte on the lips, but then he stopped.

Charlotte expecting the tender kiss opened her eyes wide and said, "What's wrong Ben? The mushrooms are making my lips dry. I think I have some lip thingy in my p-o-c-k-e-t." As she fumbled in her tight pants, Ben said, "Move your head for a second Charlotte."

Charlotte looked at Ben and said, "That's a weird thing to ask a girl when you are making out with her?"

"No. Really. There is something cool under your head. Don't you feel it?" Ben replied.

Charlotte felt the back of her head and said, "Well, Ben, there is indeed something in my hair!" and she reached behind her head and pulled out a brass lighter.

It had some initials on it, but they were so worn away it was impossible to see what letters they were. Before long Lane and Lily were interested in the investigation as well. The four were transfixed over the shiny brass object. Ben pulled out a cigarette from his pocket and flipped the lid of the lighter and a brilliant flame exploded from it. "And it works!" Ben mumbled as he lit his cigarette and took a long puff. The four sat in silence on the grass and looked out onto the city of Providence. Lane passed around the cigarette and they all took a puff until it was gone.

You guys ever gone through the tunnel?" Ben asked.

"I heard it's creepy." Charlotte said. "Can I see that lighter again?"

Ben handed it over to her, and Charlotte turned it over and over again in her hand.

"It's so pretty." She laid her head back down in the grass and watched it move trails over her head.

"I'd like to check it out." Lily said laying her head on Lane's shoulder.

"We can use the lighter to light the way!" Charlotte exclaimed.

"Okay, Chief!" Ben said pulling her up on to her skates.

It seemed dead, quiet and dark. The streets were devoid of anything or anyone. Charlotte lead the way into the entrance of the tunnel with one hand holding up the lighter in the air and her other hand holding on to Ben's. They moved in the dark for what seemed like forever. Then, there in the middle of the tunnel was a full-fledged party going on, music, lights, and a whole mess of people dancing with glow-in-the-dark sticks. They rolled on in and soon were lost among the crowd of people. Someone handed them some glow sticks to hang on their necks. As they skate-danced around, trails circled the ever-moving crowd of people. It seemed like all of Providence was in that tunnel. They even spotted some local celebrities Nick Shelby, the famous artist, and Gretchen, from the band *Sister Eleven*. What were the odds of that? It seemed like the tunnel was some weird vortex in the city of Providence.

Charlotte and Lily lost sight of their guys but they were having fun. They couldn't stop laughing. They soon found Doug and they all started dancing and sweating.

"You wouldn't *believe* who I kissed tonight?" Doug said smiling under his gaudy red lipstick. His red lips danced like the Cheshire cat from Alice in Wonderland, at times attached to his body, and other times not.

"Man, your lips aren't attached to your face. Kind of." Lily said slowly.

"Don't you want to know ladies? Aren't you dying to know who *I* kissed?" Doug asked with his hands on his hips.

"Um, please tell because we have *NO* idea, and then I can tell you who *I* kissed!" Charlotte said excitedly.

"So selfish, Charlotte. Thee James Nicolar." Doug said with a smile.

"No way! *He* was here too?" Lily exclaimed. "Shit, *everyone* is here. Cool."

"Um. Where is he now?" Charlotte asked. "I'd *love* to meet him and verify this story."

"He had to go. Off to a fab party someone was throwing for him elsewhere; In Edgar Allen Poe's old apartment. Secret party!" Doug exclaimed.

"Wow." Charlotte and Lily replied at the same time.

"Ladies your eyes are like quarters, let's dance. Nothing better than dancing on mushrooms." Doug said dragging them out to the impromptu dance floor. The dance floor comprised of a canvas painted with patterns of etcher like images that took your eyes in and out of a timeless space in day glow paint. You had a great view looking down any way you looked. On the dance floor there was a wash of sounds that made the tunnel feel large and then small at times, as if it moving around them. Charlotte and Lily felt their bodies being energized by some unknown force. The tunnel seemed electric, and the lights flashed in time with the people and the neon hanging around their necks. Doug was dancing so hard his wig soon fell off and his dress ripped at the shoulder, but he was dancing like he couldn't stop dancing. His whole body dripped with sweat. Charlotte and Lily called him "slippery man." Then he stopped and sat down in the middle of the dance floor.

"Get up!" The girls screamed at him, laughing so hard they both fell over.

"I'm so thirsty." Doug said. "Let's go find some water or something. Before I faint."

Charlotte and Lily escorted Doug on a quest for drinks. The quest led them out the end of the tunnel to the RISD Graphic Design Building.

"Vending machines." Lily said on a mission. "God, I'm so thirsty too! Good call Doug. We might have died of dehydration if we kept going."

The three of them sat down next to the vending machine drinking orange soda.

"Oh my god! This is *so* good!" Doug said.

"*So* good." Charlotte said.

"*Amazing,*" Lily replied.

"I can draw in the air check it out." Lily said.

"Me too." Doug said.

"Cool." Charlotte said.

The three of them sat there drawing in the air silently.

"I think this is my best work ever." Doug said out loud.

"Me too." Charlotte and Lily replied at the same time.

"Shit! Ben!" Charlotte said suddenly. "Get up. Man, you know how I have lusted after him. Must go find Ben!"

"What about Ben? Something happen I don't know about Charlotte?" Doug said, "How could you keep that from me, bitch. I tell *you* everything!"

"No time Doug! Got to get to him!" Charlotte screamed.

"Okay! Okay!" Doug said as he jogged in his high heels next to the girls. "It's hard to run in these things you know!" Doug said as he slowed down and fell behind the girls.

Charlotte and Lily skated slowly into the dark tunnel, as Doug wobbled behind them. They walked and they walked and they walked.

"Well. Look at that" Lily said. "I mean how long were we gone? A few minutes right?"

"I'm coming, ladies! Don't freak!" Doug yelled up to them as he swiveled on his heels. The sound echoing off the ceilings.

When Doug caught up with Charlotte and Lily he saw what they saw and said, "The party is over? We missed it? *Ugh!*"

"I heard this tunnel was haunted. Crazy shit goes on in here. My friend Dale, he's from Providence, told me." Lily said dreamily. "And it's Halloween!"

All three stood in silence inside the tunnel.

"And it's Halloween. Right. Maybe there wasn't even a party here at all? Maybe we dreamed the whole thing" Lily philosophized. "But, look at that," continued quietly as she picked up something from the ground.

"It's the lighter Ben found!" Charlotte exclaimed.

They skated around each other like little girls admiring the shiny brass lighter that Charlotte held in her hands.

"Maybe the party was further up in the tunnel?" Lily asked dreamily.

They all felt sure of it.

Charlotte led the way with the lighter. The three of them made their way through to the other side of the tunnel but there was nothing there. The party was gone. The tunnel was empty. No evidence on the ground. No trash, no discarded neon objects, no cigarettes, absolutely nothing. No one to be seen for miles, and the sun was coming up. They were so confused. *Had they been gone longer than they thought? Or was it all a dream? Was it the drugs?* They stood outside the entrance of the tunnel with their silent thoughts.

In front of them the sun was rising and it wasn't long before the party in the tunnel seemed like a world away. Perhaps, it was only a dream or a vision on the drugs in their bodies. The only thing that was important now was the Sun—and it was bursting with purples and oranges. They all stood silently next to each other watching the sky. The mushrooms were wearing off but the sunset was still a remarkable thing to see, orange, red, and purple streaks in the sky. A scene that was exploding with color as the sun was moving slowly upwards to shed its warm light on the city of Providence.

"Wish I could paint that." Doug said.

"Me too." Charlotte said.

"Let's do it." Lily said dreamily.

"With what?" Doug laughed and yawned.

"With this!" Charlotte exclaimed holding out the lighter.

"Are you still tripping?" Doug asked. "Mine has totally worn off."

"I dunno." Lily said dreamily. "Can't tell what's real and what's not. Feels like a dream and real."

Lily held the lighter in front of her and lit it and began to paint the sky. Doug and Charlotte snuggled closely to watch Lily's graceful movements against the artistic ever-changing sunrise that was evolving before them. Still not knowing what was real and what had been a dream, but knowing either way it was an experience they would never forget.

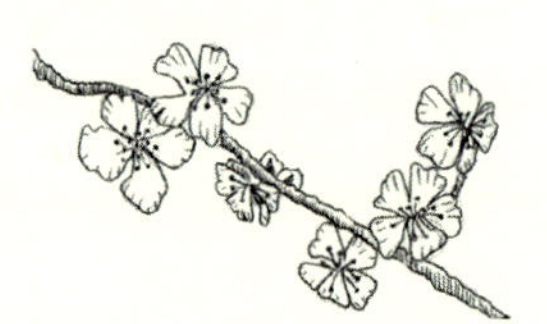

Never Date an Artist

Anna was a feminist, raised by two mothers, a lawyer and a lobbyist in Washington, D.C. Anna had always been an intelligent curious girl, and her acceptance to Brown had seemed her inevitable destiny. Anna's two mothers had brought her up to be a well-rounded person. They believed in educating Anna as a whole person. Anna excelled in school, read like a fiend, played soccer, was a black belt in karate, and generally a happy child. At Brown she was studying law. Anna was part of the law review where she had met most of her closest friends at Brown. All similar A type women who knew what they wanted it life. They had great dinner parties where they had intellectual debates, drank wine, and somehow the late night conversation always turned to why they couldn't find a good guy to date. When it came to dating, Anna's mothers had told her to: *make sure the guy treats you right, and if he doesn't he isn't worth it. A woman does not need a man to validate herself.* Anna's girlfriends had been raised on the same advice and all were fearless women, who seemed to be forever single.

Anna had found her schedule almost too busy to be bothered with dating, but a few times she inadvertently found herself on one. When a business major named Brad invited her to an entrepreneurial workshop with the Groupon creator, Anna hoped it would be a different kind of date. Brad had a great sense of humor and he and Anna had always had a laugh hanging out when she ran into him with her girlfriends at parties. Brad was relatively handsome (even though *this* had never been a high requisite on Anna's list), blonde hair, green eyes, and extremely smart. The workshop was fun and Brad made her laugh in his car all the way to restaurant with his lawyer jokes. He had had made a reservation at LaGrange and he was a gentleman holding doors for her at the restaurant entrance, although she felt he had gone a bit too far when he pulled out her chair and waited for her to sit. As Anna perused the menu she glanced up at Brad who was busy folding his napkin on his lap and arranging the fork and knife on the table so everything looked perfect. A small quirk, little OCD perhaps, but Anna was careful not to judge so soon into the evening. Anna excused herself to the bathroom and within the five short minutes she had left the table Brad had changed.

Anna searched around for the menus, and when she asked with a laugh, "Brad, did the waitress steal our menus while I was in the bathroom?"

Brad looked confused, and then responded deadpanned, "I ordered for you— a hangar steak on a bed of greens. The Pinot Grigio will go perfectly with that."

Anna was confused and shocked and thought to herself: *Who does this kind of shit? This isn't the 1800s?*

Before Anna could process the waitress placed the basket of Seven Stars bread on the table with a plate of olive oil dip. Hunger got the best of her. Anna realized she hadn't eaten since breakfast, so she devoured a piece of bread and observed this new Brad. When the appetizer of Oysters came Anna picked one up and sucked it down. Brad had a look of disgust on his face and raised his hand and whistled for the waitress.

Simultaneously Brad said, "Anna put that down. Look at the bed of lettuce it's on. It's old."

Anna laughed, "Are you serious?" Anna could see nothing wrong with the lettuce. It looked perfect to her.

"There is dirt on this leaf." Brad said to Anna pointing to the tinniest speck of dirt that was at the end of the leaf.

"It's organic dirt." Anna said with a laugh. "Here I'll rinse it off for you." She said taking a drop of her water glass and rinsing off the leaf.

Brad did not laugh, and turned to the waitress who had arrived at the table with a smile, "How can I help you Sir?"

"This lettuce is filthy. Please return it to the kitchen and bring us a new plate." Brad said all this handing the plate and not even looking at the waitress.

Anna looked at Brad in disbelief. This was turning into something out of a bad movie.

As Brad began to get drunk, the date went from bad to worse. Brad started making fun of the waiters and waitresses who worked at the restaurant and saying how much better *they* were then them—being at Brown, being rich. Brad was beginning to turn into a monster—like Dr. Jekyll and Mr. Hyde. Their food arrived and Anna seethed as she forced down her Hangar steak barely tasting anything, and then gulped her wine to get it down her throat. All Anna wanted was to run, but her body was famished and she needed to feed it. The check came, and her hunger finally subsided. Brad insisted on paying for her and for once she didn't argue. Anna excused herself to the bar saying she saw someone she wanted to say hi to. Thankfully, it was crowded enough in the restaurant by now, that she didn't have to worry about pretending. Anna ducked behind a group of people and seeing Brad unaware happily drinking his wine, she turned to the person next to her and asked, "I've never been here before does this place have a back door exit?"

"You trying to ditch your bill?" the guy replied.

"Bad date." Anna said smiling back at the guy who turned out to be quite handsome.

"Nick." He said.

"Anna." And then continued, "So, Nick. Can you get me out of here?"

"I'd be honored." Nick said with a smile and then grabbed her hand and pulled her through the crowded room to a backdoor that led into an alley. The door slammed shut behind them and they both stood in a narrow brick alleyway between the restaurant and the building next door. They stood in silence as they were total strangers in sudden close proximity to each other. Anna broke the silence first.

"Thanks Nick." Anna said with a smile.

"Your welcome, Anna." Nick said smiling and leaning

against the brick wall behind him. "Where you headed now, rebel?"

"I'm just gonna go…" The image of a guy on a poster behind Nick on the brick wall caught her eye. "Hey, that's you!"

"It is." Nick smiled, his blue eyes seeming to catch the light from the street lamp.

Anna thought, wow, he is *really* handsome.

It read, *back from his Japanese tour Nick Shelby presenting his latest painting series.*

"Maybe you can come?" Nick asked as he pointed to the poster.

She replied, "Probably not, but thanks. Not a big art person. Sorry, but *super* cool that you went to Japan. You must be good. Any chance you could help me find a cab?"

Nick hailed a cab for Anna, and said, "If you change your mind about art come on down. Here is an invite to the after party." Nick handed her a small card and waved goodbye as the cab drove off.

Anna stared at the image of Nick and smiled. The ride was long. It was a Saturday night and Providence was hopping. The streets were filled with college girls in short dresses and tall heels stumbling drunkenly down the streets. Anna watched for a while, and then stared down at the card in her hand. The picture of Nick didn't do him justice. He was much more handsome in real life. An artist? She had been warned about artists. Not from her mothers, but other girls. Her friends referred to them as "con" artists. Looking for someone to help them take care of them. Looking for a free ride. But Nick…seemed different. And after all he hadn't sought her out? She had been the one to seek him? *Well. Maybe she might go. A night with some artists wouldn't be so crazy. He was really handsome, and a gentlemen so far as she could tell. Maybe he was different. After all he had helped her out of a very bad night.* She thought to herself.

Anna *did* show up to Nick's show, but with a girlfriend, just so Nick wouldn't get the wrong idea. Within a month, much to her own surprise, she *was* dating an artist. Nick was so different from any guy she'd ever met. Nick showed up a half hour late in his beat up primer grey sedan. But Anna didn't mind. She was with Nick and he was *so* wonderful. They listened to music on his stereo. They stopped to pick up his friend Raina and her boyfriend Dale, and drove to the infamous "Railroad Bridge of Providence", a bridge straight to the sky. Anna wasn't one for taking drugs, but she hadn't been one for caring about art either. Since she had started dating Nick she had done both. The four of them got stoned in Nick's car, and then Nick led the way up to the perfect ninety-degree angle structure that sat on the grass in front of his car. Anna stared up at the strange structure that pierced the night sky with shiny patterns of moon reflections decorating it like a giraffe's neck.

"The Railroad Bridge" looked like a climb, but the moon was full and Anna was stoned, and off she went again with Nick; their relationship seemed to be always taking Anna somewhere new. It was exciting. She didn't know what would happen next. Anna liked that feeling very much. It made her feel alive. She concentrated as hard as she could on Nick's body up ahead of her, and where she was moving next. Anna felt an amazing rush as she climbed. She placed her hands and feet wherever Nick had been.

She could still feel the warmth of his hands on the rusty rails, or at least it felt like she could. Maybe it was the pot.

They climbed and climbed straight up towards the sky. Nick made it to the top, and leaned against the top rails waiting for Anna. She made it to the top, and Nick reached down and helped her up the rest of the way. Anna leaned against the rail, across from Nick.

"Raina! Dale!" Nick shouted down. "Come up! Best view in town and your missing it!"

Silence.

"I bet they're making out in my car." Nick said with a laugh. "Those guys can't get off each other!" He said. "Cool place, huh."

Anna smiled and looked out into the dark. She could just make out the river flowing below the bridge, and the currents moving the water in swirling dark patterns that reflected the light from the power plants in the distance. It was strangely silent except for the swish of cars flying by on the highway.

"Feels like you are in some sci-fi movie. Only person left in the world." Nick continued. "I used to come here alone and just sit and think. No one to yell at you, no one to think you're weird. You can just be."

Anna looked at Nick with surprise. He was such a sensitive person. Every time they were together it seemed he would expose a little bit more of his insides. He was like no man she had ever met, or dreamed of meeting. And he was *so* different from her.

"Is it hard just *being*, for you, Nick?" Anna asked feeling like it came out kind of awkwardly. Anna didn't want Nick to think that she pitied Nick, she just felt compelled to ask him why. Anna was just trying to understand him. This artist named "Nick" that just had happened to cross paths with her accidentally one day on a bad datc was so complex.

"Sometimes." Nick started, and then paused.

"I'm sorry, Nick. I didn't mean that to come out the way it did." Anna said.

There was a strange awkward silence that you usually feel between strangers—they had only been together for a month. All of a sudden it felt like a much shorter time, and a little distance widened between the two of them. Anna saw a change come over Nick's face as he said, "My father, when I lived at home, he used me as his punching bag, that's how I got this permanent twist in my nose. Like it?" Nick said as he turned his nose to the side to show her. More silence. Anna wasn't sure what to say. She didn't know *anyone* who had been beaten up by parents. That just wasn't the world she had grown up in. Nick smiled at her, and Anna smiled back. Somehow Nick's smile lightened the mood, albeit briefly.

"That was for being in the way of him and my mom." He continued and then lit up a cigarette.

Nick was so different. He was like a gentleman from a long time ago, except in a modern way. He treated Anna like a woman in the right ways, and didn't patronize her in the wrong ways. Yet, they were so different. Nick glanced over the side of the railing and smoked looking out in the direction of the lights flickering at the power plants. Anna hadn't noticed his nose, but it made her like him even more. Nick was like a character out of the romantic Jane Austin novels she'd liked so much growing up. Nick was a deep, gentle, and kind soul. He was handsome, but his kind ways and big heart was what she loved. The guys she'd dated never opened up like this to her. In fact, she had so little patience with most men, having been raised by two strong intellectual women, she found most guys just boring and dull. Sure, there may have been an initial sense of attraction, but then just a lot of stupid guy things Anna never respected. Nick wasn't like that at all. He was quiet and thoughtful, and he was sharing something with her. It was silent and peaceful up on the bridge. Anna felt like they were the only people in the world.

"He broke my collarbone too. See my shoulder it isn't even." Nick said as he pulled his t-shirt down, to expose a little bump where the bone was out of place and trying to poke it's way through the skin. The sudden shock of seeing his skin under the moonlight in her stoned state was mesmerizing.

"Shit! Is your father in jail?" Anna asked.

This made Nick laugh. She laughed too. Somehow, it seemed okay to laugh.

"Yep. Big court case and then my uncle took me in. It doesn't hurt. Just feels out of place sometimes. I'm pretty used to it now. My mother died when I was five. Car accident." Nick said blowing out smoke and giving a shrug. "Shit. I've never said out loud to anyone. Pretty fucked up, right? Nick Shelby's glorious past."

"I'm sorry." Anna said feeling helpless. She was from a world of safe nurturing. Nick was breaking her heart, and making Anna fall in love with him at the same time. All in one tiny moment and it was almost too much for Anna. Nick was being so open and honest with her already in such a short time.

"I feel comfortable with you Anna. It's kind of funny. I don't really talk about that shit with anyone. Usually." Nick said with a smile.

Anna smiled back not knowing what to say back but feeling the girl in her surge with hormonal giddiness.

"You know, can I say how refreshing it is to date a girl that didn't know who I was when they met me." Nick said with a smile. "I hope that doesn't sound conceited. Just hard to trust anyone's intentions."

"Well, I might have figured it out with all those posters around town, but unless you hadn't save me from that horrible date, I might have read about you somewhere, but you know art, not being my comfort zone, not on my radar, I guess." Anna said flatly.

They stood in silence a little longer. Anna liked the simultaneous silence and company. It was like having a good book and a warm blanket in your favorite chair. Nick stirred in her adventure, poetry, and things she'd never experienced before in real life, only in high literature. Nick started talking about silly stoner things he noticed about the bridge, and Anna started laughing uncontrollably. Dancing around the heavy conversation they were having shortly before. Nick did the job of breaking the heaviness and they were two stoners again hanging up on the top of a railroad bridge together.

"Hey, I can see you blushing even in this darkness. It's so cute, Anna." Nick said as reached his hand out and touched Anna's face.

Then he grabbed her hand and pulled her close to him, and

started kissing her with the sweetest passionate kisses she had ever been the recipient of. Anna felt faint like she might just fall off the rails into the river below at any moment. Anna felt herself fall into his kiss. She never wanted the feeling of his sweet lips to leave hers. But then he pulled back stared at Anna and smiled. She felt Nick's arms holding her tight. She gave into him completely.

"Nick Shelby, you are so dreamy." Anna said.

"And Anna you are soooo stoned." Nick said with a laugh.

Then Nick stopped and wrapped his arms around her, and turned her to the direction of the sunrise. Anna stood there leaning against his warm body, feeling the sun's rays reaching them far below its orbit, and the sun felt comforting on her face, and Nick felt so good.

"You are beautiful Anna." Nick whispered in her ear.

And for that moment Anna did indeed feel beautiful. She felt like a work of art. Like Nick's work of art.

Their relationship blossomed, but over time Anna "the muse" began to really start bothering Anna "the independent-feminist-lawyer-rule the-world-young-woman" she'd always been. Nick was like no man she'd ever thought she could possibly meet. Yet, lately Anna would leave him feeling a sense of lingering doubt. Thoughts that had never run through her head before began filling up the invincible strong neurons in her left sided brain to feel pushed as far to the right side as she could possibly imagine. *Am I turning into a groupie? Am I supposed to give up my dreams and life to be with Nick? Am I going to spend the rest of my life following the famous Nick Shelby around the world? What am I going to be cooking and cleaning for a famous artist the rest of my life? This might be romantic to some other girl but what the hell??? Could a girl really have it all?*

Nick's travels began to take him away more and more—Israel, Europe, and Australia. He was away more than he was around and Anna's life ironically returned to its normal sensible routine. When Nick was gone her life made sense. Anna missed Nick, but she also treasured her freedom and independence. After all, her whole life had been on a certain path for so long, to hinge and change it for a man? That went against everything she had been raised to be. It stood opposite of everything she had been taught to be. Anna's time with Nick was wonderful, but scary too. What made Anna more confused about the whole Nick thing were her two mothers. Nick came and spent Christmas at Anna's house and Anna's mothers had just simply fallen in love with Nick. It was all *so* wrong. If anyone should have objected to her falling in love with an artist, it should have been her two intellectual mothers! But no, they thought Nick was charming, talented, and so in love with Anna. They tried explaining to her how they saw Anna through Nick's eyes in a new way. Somehow Anna had left that vacation angry. Anna had hoped her mothers would clear her head and put her back on the straight path she had always known. Career, intelligence, and smart, smart, smart decisions. She had *never* before strayed from that path.

Every time Nick came home and showed up with flowers. All those things Anna had been told to ignore all her logical life, she simply couldn't. Anna fell back in love with Nick every time. Anna felt herself falling and it felt scary and yet wonderful all at the same time. Perhaps, for the moment, Anna would go with this as if it was a phase. This was Anna's rebellious moment she would laugh about with her children. As a future successful lawyer, her children would never believe, she, *their* mother, had been Nick Shelby's muse. Perhaps, she could just for the moment relax, and enjoy the moment. And in Nick's kiss, she believed she could.

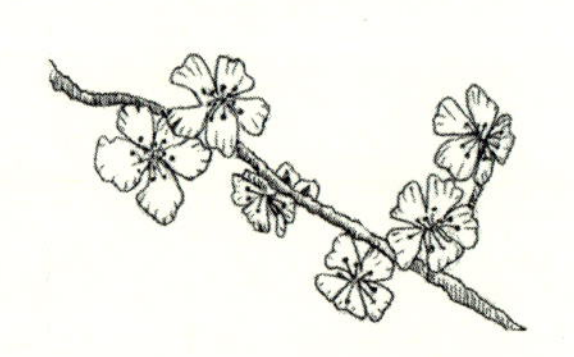

Do You Know My Name?

Gretchen's mother was a former Miss Rhode Island. Gretchen's mother was always self-involved, and when her own beauty began to fade with age she turned to Gretchen to fill the emptiness. Gretchen's mother entered her in beauty contests and for a while Gretchen put up with the hair, makeup, clothes—being made to look like a little doll. She put up with turning when told, smiling on cue, and moving like a model. Most of the time she was happy to please her mother and make her smile. After all every girl wants approval from her mother, right? Gretchen went along with it all until middle school. Everything changed. Well doesn't everything change then? Like breasts, private parts, hormones, zits, feelings, boys, boys, boys, and jealous girls.

Girls hated Gretchen in school because she was so pretty and the boys wouldn't leave her alone. She didn't want to end up like her mother but she wasn't sure how to deal with it all. So that's when she started not eating. It was the only thing she could control. She knew it was wrong, but she was so angry and she had no way to express it. Everything was going as planned. Gretchen was *completely* in control. Everything was in control until...Gretchen passed out in school and ended up in the hospital. When she came out of the hospital, she started seeing a therapist, and she had to talk about why she had done what she did. Her therapist was cool and Gretchen felt relieved to finally be able to express herself. Gretchen's therapist suggested playing an instrument or joining a club to help her ease back into a social life. That was the year she discovered the power of playing the electric guitar. Gretchen dyed her hair pink and cut it short. She learned as many of her favorite songs as she could, The Ramones, The Rolling Stones, The Clash, and even some Neil Young. Gretchen felt free of the beauty chains that had messed with her head as a child. She ditched it all...boys, breasts, prettiness, sex, hate, love, and hormones. She traded it all in for rock and roll.

After many years of struggling to play and sing, playing in punk bands, ska bands, and rock bands, her rock and roll training had paid off. She finally had her own band—*Sister Eleven.* In the Providence music scene her guitar abilities made her stand out. As much as she tried to hide her beauty it shone through when she was onstage. Soon *Sister Eleven* were the buzz of Providence, and people began to take notice from as far away

as Boston and New York. *Sister Eleven*'s first recordings traveled the blog circuit. Word of mouth went viral. They got invited to play on the tiny desk concert NPR and Daytrotter.

Gretchen and her band were playing bigger shows and she was soon traveling to places like London. Gretchen tried to hold it together. She wasn't about to lose her head over this thing. She was smart enough to know that this could all disappear tomorrow and she might have to start over again and get a real job. However, lately, a few things had begun to feel a bit out of her control, and she was doing her best to figure out how to handle it. Unlike her eating disorder the rules seemed harder to follow. The other guys in her band all looked to her to deal with the big decisions. She was the star and the bandleader. Sometimes, it was hard, but Gretchen knew she was good at this, and this was her chance to do what she loved for a living. She wasn't about to blow that on purpose.

Gretchen had recently taken a trip to New York to listen to the final mastering of their record, and while the music sounded fantastic, they had done so much to her voice that she didn't like. Gretchen felt caught between wanting to make a stink, and not wanting to come across as a complaining rock star. Gretchen felt conflicted. She felt like a cog in the machine. The record company was happy, so why shouldn't she be as well? If they thought they could sell it, perhaps, she should just allow them to. A week later, she had her answer I guess. The first single was a hit, 48,000 likes on day one. I guess she would just go with the flow and trust these record people. Perhaps, they *did* know what they were doing after all. She would have to wait and see.

One of the ways she tried keeping herself grounded was

maintaining a close friendship with her friend Nick Shelby, who also happened to be in the same situation as her. They had always been friends, never had any funny romantic stuff between them, just a sense of respect for the art that was their lives, Gretchen's music, and Nick's art. She had met Nick when they were really young before either of them had a taste of all this craziness that surrounded them both. Gretchen had gone to Hank's Tattoo Shop in downtown Providence for her first tattoo, and Nick was working at the front desk. They were both fifteen years old. Nick had been there for her when Gretchen was going through her bulimia. Gretchen had passed out in front of the shop and it was Nick who saved her life. Nick had come down every day to visit her in the hospital and then when she went off to the Eating Disorders Clinic. So now, he was really the *only* person she trusted.

Gretchen arrived back in town off her tour opening up for the band *Crash Crazy* one of the biggest up-and-coming bands in America at the moment. Nick asked her to play a few songs at a party he was throwing. As tired as she was, there was no way she would refuse him. Nick had been there for her since the beginning. Nick had believed in Gretchen before anyone else cared, and that meant the world to Gretchen. Gretchen played a few songs and then made her rounds at the party telling everyone about her tour with *Crash Crazy*.

Soon however Gretchen started feeling that sense of being overwhelmed by the attention and having to talk so much about herself. Gretchen turned around looking for a way out and saw a girl standing near her by herself. Gretchen looked at the girl, and noticed she stood out from the rest of Nick's party scene. She was dressed in jeans and a t-shirt, but the jeans were brand new, and her t-shirt was neatly tucked into her jeans. Her medium brown hair was pulled simply into a low ponytail.

Gretchen turned to the girl to ask for a light but before she could say the words the girl quickly spat out, "Nick went out to buy get some beer, but he will back soon."

Gretchen replied with a laugh, "Oh, I was just gonna see if *you* had a cigarette."

The girl replied, "*Oh. Me????*"

"Gretchen." She said holding her hand out to the girl.

The girl shook her hand and smiled.

"And you are?" Gretchen asked.

"Oh. Yeah. Me. Anna." The girl replied shaking Gretchen's hand.

"Well, Anna. Do you?" Gretchen asked.

"Do I?" Anna asked looking confused.

Gretchen laughed and continued, "Have a cigarette?"

"Oh. No. Sorry. I don't smoke." Anna replied.

Gretchen noticed that the girl Anna didn't wear much makeup at all, just a little pink lipstick and some blush. Gretchen thought that was a relief from all the gaudy makeup she'd witnessed earlier in the evening amongst the artsy crowd at Nick's party.

"I saw you play earlier. Big fan." Anna said quickly looking down. Ann's face turned bright red.

"Oh, thanks." Gretchen replied smiling at the cuteness of Anna and her honesty showing through on her face.

"Hey gals. See you have met." Nick said with a smile as he

walked up to the two girls.

"Yeah." Gretchen said with a smile. "But I'm *really* curious as to how the two of you know each other Nick.

"My girlfriend." Nick said putting his arm around Anna.

"*Ahh*. Cool." Gretchen said. "She told me you were out on a run for beer. You got anything good? And a ciggie for me?"

Nick handed her a beer and a pack of cigarettes out of a plastic bag. As soon as he was ready to take a sip of his beer Nick was being pulled away by a group of giggling artsy chicks.

Gretchen pulled out a cigarette and lit it, and watched Anna's face change from a smile to discomfort.

"You hungry Anna?" Gretchen asked.

"What?" Anna asked looking confused at Gretchen.

"Eat. Want to eat, and also escape this party for a while?" Gretchen asked with a smile.

"Yes." Anna said looking back at Nick being fawned on.

"Gets kind of annoying, huh?" Gretchen asked.

"A little." Anna said. "I mean I'm happy for him; just not sure why I came? I could have easily stayed at home with a good book. I don't mind."

Gretchen smiled at Anna and said, "I *do* know. Now, let's get out of here."

"I'm taking your girlfriend with me I will drop her off later." Gretchen said as she and Anna passed Nick on the way out. Nick waved from the crowd that surrounded him.

Gretchen and Anna drove to Haven Brothers downtown. Gretchen loved Haven Brothers. It was an icon in Providence. There was something comforting about the diner still being around after all these years. Gretchen and Anna sat down on the sidewalk and ate hotdogs on paper plates.

Gretchen said, "Shit, I am so sick of talking about myself. Anna tell me about you?"

"You want to know about me? Kind of boring." Anna replied taking a sip of her coke.

"Yep." Gretchen replied placing her tray on sidewalk and lighting a cigarette.

"I go to Brown. Going to be a lawyer. I have two moms." Anna said with a smile.

"Cool. *Very* cool." Gretchen said. "I *knew* you were different when I met you."

Anna looked taken aback.

"Go on. I interrupted you," Gretchen said. "I'll smoke. You talk."

Anna smiled and continued: "Well, I met Nick trying to escape a bad date."

"*Ooh,* this is going to be good. Do tell. I love hearing about bad dates." Gretchen said scooting closer to Anna.

"I had this awful date with this business guy named Brad. *Ugh.* Even if his name fits him! It was awful! He ordered for me when I left the table. He did all these stupid guy things trying to impress me that only made me hate him. Nothing intellectually stimulating about Brad!" Anna stopped and said, "This must sound so stupid to you, traveling around, meeting celebrities."

"No way, Anna." Gretchen said, "Continue."

"Anyway, I went to the bar to get away from him for a moment, and then decided I needed to get the hell out of there as soon as I could. I'd never done that before." Anna continued looking thoughtful.

"That's so awesome Anna! So Punk rock!" Gretchen exclaimed and giving her a punch in her arm.

"Well, I turned to the person next to me at the bar, it was Nick, and asked if he knew of a back entrance. And off we went. Then, he invited me to his art show. I mean I didn't know anything about art. Lawyer type, but I decided to go. I don't know why. Well, and now it's been a month, and…" Anna paused.

"Yes…And…" Gretchen continued looking eagerly at Anna.

"I think I'm kind of falling in love with the guy." Anna finished smiling. "Ah, I feel incredibly stupid saying that out loud.

Gretchen smiled and said, "Cool."

Gretchen looked at Anna and smiled. She could tell Anna didn't love Nick for being famous, she *really* loved him, well, for him. Gretchen, thought*: maybe it is possible after all. If Nick could find someone like this, maybe there is hope for me.*

They sat in silence and watched some college kids stumble drunkenly making fools out of themselves outside of Haven Brothers. Gretchen and Anna both looked at each other and started laughing. It was entertaining, and you never knew whom you would run into at Haven Brothers. It attracted every sort of person from Providence seeking late night greasy food.

"There's something I've been meaning to ask you. There is a rasp in your voice that I don't hear on the record." Anna said.

Gretchen, said, "I can't believe you notice that Anna." Gretchen looked at Anna. "I *knew* there was something different about you. Yeah, they cleaned my vocals saying that the vocals didn't have to be so interesting because my photo on the record cover would sell records."

"Well, the record is still awesome. And for what it's worth, you are always great live. I like your music for the guttural rawness of it. It wouldn't matter what you looked like; it's real. It would still be as big as it is." Anna finished.

"Thanks Anna." Gretchen smiled. "That *really* means a lot to me. You don't even *know* how much. Now, I probably should be getting you home." The two girls smiled at each other.

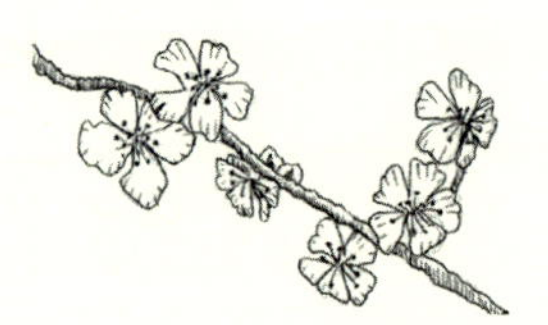

It's Just Stupid Clay

Letti stared out the window and then down at two white pills in her hand. Two perfectly round white circles with an inscription of letters that read the name of the company that made the pill. Letti felt the indentations of the letters with her fingertips. Her fingernails clinically short enough now that her skin felt raw as it touched the pills. The pills seemed so innocuous and yet held so much power. Letti hated those pills, but the nurse in front of her would not leave until she had swallowed them. Letti heard classical music in the background coming from the hallway. *Music to soothe the patients* she thought to herself. It was all so stereotypical of what one thought of as a loony bin. Letti wanted to laugh at it all, but then the joke was only on her. She was *in* the loony bin—and *that* was nothing to laugh about. Letti's experience with classical music had been fancy theaters with gold-tiered balconies and a conductor in his elegant black suit. That classical music was civilized and refined. Butler

Hospital with its hard tiled white floors, white ceilings, white walls, and white nurse uniforms was sanitized. Free of any character, culture, and very much closed to the outside world.

The nurse on call stood in front of her waiting patiently for Letti to swallow the pills and hand her the paper cup of water she was holding gently between the tips of her delicate fingers painted a cheery pink color. Letti envied the nurse. She could have color in her life. The nurse's nails were the only color in a sea of whiteness around Letti. The nurse was pretty with curly blonde hair and a warm smile that matched her hot pink nails. Letti swallowed the pills and drank the water, and the nurse said, "Rest up, Letti," and gently guided Letti's head down on to the pillow. This happened every day over and over again—for how long, she didn't know.

Letti's eyes followed the nurse as she exited through the doorway and then moved across to her sleeping roommate who had already taken her pills for the day and was fast asleep. Since Letti had been here, her roommate had been asleep. Letti had yet to see her awake and officially meet her. Letti knew her name from the plate on the door she passed each time she went to a different doctor, meeting, or activity. Her name was Rachel Wisk and they had shared a sleeping space for some time but never met. Time didn't make sense in this place, and there were no clocks anywhere. The doctor's and nurses wore watches on their wrists, but there was never an opportunity to see the face of a clock when you were a patient. It made Letti so angry. There was no control. What she wanted so badly was to control things again. The medicine made that impossible. She felt like Alice In Wonderland having fallen down that rabbit hole and everywhere she went nothing made any sense to her.

Time was different here. It was managed by people coming and going; instead of hours, minutes, and seconds on a clock. Perhaps, Rachel was awake when she slept and stared across wondering when Letti would awake. Her roommate had bandages on her arms and wrists and Letti could just slightly make out a little trace of bloodstains underneath the bandages. That's how Letti's

mind was in this place—Like a microscope looking for details and things that were hidden. Letti's brain desired anything to cure her boredom of this place. Letti was used to fine restaurants, boarding schools, and Shakespearean plays. It was her senior year of High School and this *should* have been the best year ever for her. What had gone wrong? Her psychiatrist kept mentioning her parents and their recent divorce, but Letti never cared about her parents staying together. Letti didn't care that her father had cheated on her mother. That was *their* problem. What did that have to do with her? Letti barely saw them anyway, the amount they traveled. Her father was a psychiatrist, and had been the one to officially commit her to Butler Hospital when the boarding school had called informing of Letti's state. Apparently she had locked herself in her room and destroyed the place over a series of three days. The official report said that she hadn't slept or eaten in four days. Her roommate had finally told the RA on her. She had been carried out strapped to a board. Her mother had been away in Tahiti on a spa vacation.

At school she had a great group of friends. Everyone thought Letti was super smart and she excelled in all of her classes. Letti was going to be the Valedictorian, and had received an early acceptance to Brown University. There was her one dirty secret—throwing up in the bathroom. Only her friend Gretchen suspected. Gretchen had come into the bathroom once when Letti was vomiting. Letti had told Gretchen that she had a bug and wasn't feeling well. But then Gretchen commented on how thin she was getting lately, and that she was worried about her. Letti would always brush it off and give her some story like, "Must be all those pilates I've been doing lately." Letti didn't think she was too thin when she looked in the mirror. When Letti compared herself to the girls in magazines she thought she looked like them. Letti liked how thin she looked.

The only person who had visited her at Butler besides her parents was her friend Gretchen from boarding school. Although the visit didn't go as well as Letti had imagined. Having a visitor was exciting, and Letti had set her expectations high.

"You look good Letti." Gretchen said with a smile.

"No. *You* look good Gretchen." Letti replied, "Can you get me out of here, *please?* Sneak me out under your coat?"

They both laughed.

"I can't believe they got me holed up in here. I'm not crazy! Shit!" Letti said.

"Yeah. I know. I did this too remember? It sucks, but it's worth it. You got to do deal with your shit you know or it will literally eat you away." Gretchen said.

"I know Gretchen! Shit! Don't you think they remind me of that every second here!" Letti's voice rose.

A couple other visitors turned their heads to look at Letti.

Gretchen stayed silent.

"What?" Letti asked Gretchen. "Did I piss you off? Sorry Gretchen. I mean *I'm* the one in this place! You think you understand but you don't! Sorry to upset you and your wonderful life!"

Gretchen remained silent.

"Jesus Gretchen. At least say something! You are making me feel crazy!" Letti finished.

Gretchen handed Letti an envelope.

"When you are ready you can read it. It's a stupid card." Gretchen said and then got up and left.

Letti shoved it in her pocket. She was in no mood to read a card from Gretchen. She was angry.

Every day on Letti's schedule was "Art therapy." A happy-go-lucky lady named Ms. Zane taught the class. Letti *hated* making art. It seemed so infantile, so idiotic. Letti was not a child, and yet she felt like ever since she had come to this place she was being treated like a child everywhere. Letti was more of a high literature girl, and the drugs they'd had her on since she'd come to Butler made it impossible for her to read a sentence without straining her brain and hurting her vision. So instead, her free awake time was now shoving her once fine nails in dirty slimy clay that Ms. Zane would hand out during the group sessions. Ms. Zane was from the sixties generation, long graying hair, flowing skirts with paisleys, crystal necklaces, and all that came with being a "hippy." Ms. Zane smelled of patchouli or some all-natural products that had only fragrances from earthy things like dirt.

As Letti listened to Ms. Zane give instructions and talk, she imagined doing a full makeover on her, but then thought she would never make it past the foundation stage with these drugs in her system. At first, Letti couldn't get past the frustration of rolling long pieces of clay and trying to spiral it in a circle before it fell off or split. It made her angry. If this was supposed to help her, it wasn't doing anything but making her frustrated and angry at the stupidity of it all. Give her a large novel of a thousand pages and she could interpret the metaphors, inferences, and allegories, with the stroke of a pen. She could argue any debate as well as Plato or Socrates. Letti would deftly solve mathematical calculations with zeal and finesse. Give her Calculus, Biology, Physics, and History, she would be fine. With the clay she felt helpless, hopeless and just plain stupid.

Letti watched the other girl zombies carefully rolling their clay and spiraling them in perfect circles. All of the girls seemed to be happy and smiling, and at peace. They had drank the Koolaid, and bought it hook, line, and sinker. One day, Letti observed the girl next to her struggling with her spiral —which was headed in a lopsided direction. In solidarity she whispered, "You buying this crap?" The girl looked at Letti with a slightly annoyed expression, and said, "I think it's kind of cool." Without another word the girl returned to her clay bowl spiral that was now headed in the opposite direction. Letti looked around the room and watched the intense look of concentration on every single girls face in the room. Ms. Zane walked around with a gentle voice guiding each girl. She stopped at Letti and asked, "You okay Letti?"

"Sure." Letti said unsure of whether or not this was the truth. In this place she did *not* feel okay. She did *not* feel like herself.

This was how every Art Therapy session happened. The rest of the girls exited the room with a sense of elation, and Letti felt total defeat. Letti had never, *not* succeeded, at anything she tried, until now. Letti had always admired art from afar as something she might purchase, but never as something she felt inclined to do. She was making headway with her psychiatrist. They were digging deep into Letti's issues, her bulimia, her anxiety, and her parents. The deeper Letti was able to dig, the less drugs her psychiatrist put into her body. Soon, she began to feel like she was returning to a human. Letti was able to read again, and this gave her some solace. Letti went to the library everyday hungry for more books. The return to the rational mind and intellectual stimulation brought her a large dose of comfort to her being, but sadness still lingered deep inside her soul. That was hard to rid her self of.

Without the drugs in her body, Letti began to dream again and when she awoke they stayed vivid in her mind. Letti began to have dreams again where she was Alice in Wonderland, falling in and out of holes. She passed her parents as she fell down past tree roots; She squeezed through small doors and met up with her friend Gretchen who was kept feeding her strange objects like toys

to eat; And played croquet on the lawn of Brown with a strange woman who looked an awful lot like Ms. Zane. Everyone from her past made an appearance in her dreams in some way, but Ms. Zane was always in them handing her clay and asking her to make something complicated like the Eiffel Tower. And in her dreams she did it. She felt the smooth cold clay in her hands as she whipped up masterpiece after masterpiece. Ms. Zane would marvel at her work.

Letti's dreams had become so real that she felt the clay on her hands even after she had woke. The dreams began to have such an effect on her that she began to feel like she was changing in some way. Letti couldn't put her finger on it. Maybe this stuff was working? Maybe she was making progress? Letti smiled more and she didn't know why. In her dreams she had overcome something and she felt different. Gretchen came to visit Letti for a second time shortly after these dreams had begun to occur. When Letti found out she was coming she decided it was time to read the card she had shoved away in anger a couple months back.

Letti,

I can't imagine what you are going through. Just know that you will get through it. You are an amazing person. You have challenged me in ways you can't imagine. Here's a stupid card to make you laugh at life's sometimes stupidity. Remember to laugh at yourself when you can, so you can remind yourself you are human. You can stumble and fall. When you get up from that fall you are always looking at things from a better angle. Thanks for being a great friend to me. I hope I can do the same for you someday.

Love,

Gretchen

The center of the card was a cartoon of a girl looking sad and a bunch of animals laughing at the girl. It made Letti smile even though it made no sense. When Gretchen arrived Letti ran up to her and hugged her. It felt so good to have a real friend. They spent the afternoon talking about school life and Gretchen told her all about some recent hilarious events. Gretchen seemed to know just the right stories to tell her that would make her laugh. This time Letti didn't feel jealous, she felt apart of her life again. Gretchen told her about how a friend of theirs, Jason, had been caught in the girl's dorm room afterhours. He had run across campus carrying his clothes being chased by the RA. This had made legendary video footage. After that, a food fight had broken out in the cafeteria and the whole school had spent Saturday cleaning the cafeteria to the kitchen people's satisfaction. It was a great afternoon and when Gretchen left Letti felt like she was a teenager again. It felt good.

Letti finished her first real clay bowl outside of her dreams, just three days before she was due to be released from Butler. The rest of the girls had made several other objects out of clay in the same time it took Letti to complete one stupid bowl. And yet, upon completion of the bowl, as lopsided and ugly as it was, it made her feel different. She was proud and she wasn't sure why. The bowl seemed to be snaked together with the last couple months of everything she'd been through. Like Pandora's box, it was laced and woven with her darkest fears and secrets. It was filled with the rage, anxiety, and sadness in every coil. It felt like a reminder of how far she'd been. The day her parents arrived to pick her up, Letti stood in the lobby cradling her bowl as if it were a life raft. Somehow this stupid bowl felt like safety. She was unsure of how she would do on the outside, but looking down at her bowl she knew she had changed for better on the inside.

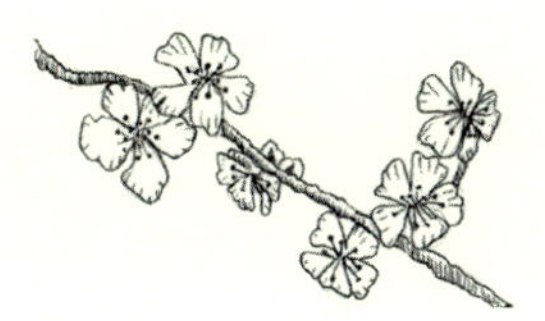

The Dadaist Collector

There is always a treasure to be found in this world. This is what Mr. Georges told all the young artists that hung out at the squatter's loft where he had been taken in by a young artist. It was a kind-hearted kid named Nick Shelby that had invited Mr. Georges in on one of the coldest nights in New England. It had snowed twenty-two inches and the temperature at night was five below zero. Mr. Georges hadn't eaten more than a frozen sandwich, slightly moldy, the day before. It was all that he had been able to pull apart from a receptacle. Nick had found Mr. Georges huddled up coughing in front of the loft looking like he was on death's door, up to his knees in snow. Perhaps, thinking back, he might have been, if it hadn't been for this kid Nick. Nick made him hot coffee and some soup that first night; and saved his life.

Mr. Georges first night in Olneyville, he took his first

real shower in over a year. The last one was at a shelter, when he thought he might come in off the streets. Mr. Georges had been homeless for two years after his third wife had kicked him out for drinking too much. Ironically, the streets sobered him up pretty fast. One could only be an alcoholic if you had the money to spend on it. He had been laid off from his job at The Smith Brothers Hardware store he had worked at for more than twenty years. The Smith family just couldn't keep up the big stores prices. They had been kind to him as an employer and they felt bad, but really there was nothing they could do. After that Mr. Georges applied to the larger chains, enduring interviews by people more than half his age. It was humiliating. The look on their young faces was always, "Sorry man, you are just too old."

He was fifty-five... fifty-five, and useless, in this modern world. He didn't know how he became an alcoholic it seemed so innocuous at first drinking on the front porch to kill the sadness. Mr. Georges' wife had a jewelry store she owned and worked every day late into the evening. Mr. Georges would shop for groceries, clean the house, and prepare the meals for his wife to eat when she got home. But it was a long day, and every one he knew worked so it was a lonely day.

When Mr. Georges stepped inside the shower stall in Olneyville, and turned the valve with his shaky hands, the water raining down on his homeless body felt like a miracle from God. Mr. Georges wasn't religious but this seemed like a miracle if there was one. A few times that first night, at the loft, he wondered if he had actually died in front of that loft out in the freezing cold and Nick was angel bringing him to heaven. Mr. Georges hadn't believed in all that stuff before, but maybe God was testing him? Maybe he was wrong not to believe? Maybe it was time to start believing? As Mr. Georges stared into the mirror that hung from a wooden hook, he saw an old man. The years Mr. Georges had lived on the street had not prepared him for this moment. It was a shock, at first, but that feeling quickly passed. He was alive and he had just showered. On the streets he had lost his ego. A mirror was only useful if you had a home to hang it in. As he pulled on the long underwear shirt over his head that Nick had given him, the feeling of the soft clean clothes made him think of his mother dressing him when he was young. It was the feeling of cleanliness, safety, and home. The sweater had some moth holes in it but it was made of wool and it was warm. Although the sweater was well worn it still felt like a warm blanket around his body. A comfort perhaps only young children and street people could appreciate. His weight loss from living on the streets had allowed his old body to easily fit in Nick's young clothes.

The first night, Mr. Georges and Nick ate a quiet meal together on a red and black diner style table, something that felt more like his time than this young man sitting in front of him. Mr. Georges admired how calm and serious the boy was for a young man. Nick seemed like an old man trapped in a young body. Mr. Georges had often felt like a young man inside an old body—that was until he became homeless. Mr. Georges ate his soup as slowly as possible. He was afraid he might get sick. Mr. Georges didn't want to scare off this kind young man that had taken him in. Vomiting on an empty stomach is not for the feint of heart, or the young. It smelled like death and old age.

"Do you mind if I draw a sketch of you?" Nick asked

"Well, why'd you want to do that son?" Mr. Georges answered gruffly wiping soup off is lip with the back of his hand.

Mr. Georges hadn't been around people for so long that speaking to people didn't come naturally. The minute the words had fallen off his lips he wished he could put them back, but he had no idea how. Survival on the streets had no need for "thank you" and other pleasantries. Mr. Georges had to tgo slow, like eating. Mr. Georges needed to enter this new world carefully. Nick, however, didn't seem to notice. Or perhaps he was too kind. *Perhaps, an angel*, Mr. Georges, thought. This all felt like a dream he would wake up from and be on the streets again out in the freezing cold. Surviving.

"You have a face filled with life." Nick said with smiling. And for the first time in awhile, Mr. Georges felt a strange sensation of something...maybe warmth? It was hard to say. Years of street living had calloused more than just his feet and hands; his heart was pretty brittle as well. Mr. Georges nodded his head, and Nick began to sketch. Mr. Georges was a good model. He could sit still. Something Mr. Georges had learned from homelessness, when you didn't want to be caught sleeping against someone's property.

Survival on the streets often meant being invisible. Which was hard when you had no home, and you smelled like death.

When Nick showed Mr. Georges the sketch of him, he felt a sense of joy he hadn't experience in a long time. There was a sense of respect shown by the portrait and something otherworldly. It was something from his church going days of his first marriage when they spoke of heaven and angels. All those babies flying in clouds looking so peaceful. All those descriptions of heaven; Art seemed to be a gift from God. "Good. Boy." Is all Mr. Georges was able to muster, but inside his heart was fluttering with a feeling of lightness and newness.

Ironically, he had felt this same heavenly feeling digging deep down in a trashcan. His hands deftly moving about moldy sandwich crusts, cigarette butts, vomit soaked napkins, and sharp bottle caps. Each glass bottle or silver can he came up with put a smile on his face. Mr. Georges ritually cleaned each one with an old shirt he'd found discarded on the street. He liked the way the bottles shone in the daylight. Mr. Georges would carefully place each glass bottle and can in his shopping cart as if it were an expensive sculpture. Somehow Mr. Georges saw these mundane items differently as a homeless man. Not only were they money to feed him and keep his old body alive, but the idea that a simple bottle or a can could literally keep him alive was something special. These items most people gave no thought to, other than the liquid they would quench their thirst with. To him, a homeless man, gold. As Mr. Georges rolled his cart along the streets he would admire the collage of colors of the different labels on the cans and bottles piled below. They even had a musical ring to them as they clinked up next to each other from the uneven movement of the cart.

After that first day the young man Nick did more than offer him a place to stay warm he offered him work. The work for Nick turned into an opportunity for some company as well; something Mr. Georges had forgotten he had missed. The work was stretching large canvases for Nick to paint on. Nick had been commissioned by an art gallery named Art Connections to have his first solo show. The day Nick got the news the first person he told was Mr. Georges. To Mr. Georges, who'd never had any children after three marriages, he imagined this is what it felt like to be a father. Mr. Georges watched the other artists clamber around Nick as if he was a rock star. Mr. Georges felt a sense of parental pride. He was different than the other young kids who hung out in the loft in Olneyville, who saw Mr. Georges as an old man, useless compared to their surging hormones and burgeoning youth that was written on their faces.

It took some time to get the hang of stretching the can-

vas material, but Mr. Georges' old plumbing skills came back to him, and food and hearth had brought some of his old strength back. When Nick did not need him he spent time reading the books in Nick's small library. He read about Salvador Dali, Eduard Manet, Rembrandt, and his favorite Duchamp. One day when Mr. Georges was cleaning the dishes in the kitchen and stacking the glasses in a perfect row on the shelf, Nick asked, "Have you ever built a sculpture?"

That one question began Mr. Georges exploration into sculpture made of found objects. His time on the street became a skill beyond survival. It now evolved into creation. Creation was a magnificent feeling that Mr. Georges never experienced. Mr. Georges knew he must have been getting good when some of the other artists began to admire his work and call him by the nickname "The Dadaist Collector." A special bond began to grow between the Nick and Mr. Georges. Like a father and son, both being drawn to each for which the other had lacked in their life. Nick had shared with Mr. George's about how his dad had beat him and his mother had died when he was young. Mr. George's told him of his lives previous to being homeless. They came up with the name of Mr. Georges first piece together during one of their late night talks. It was called "Toilet in the park" very much inspired by Marcel Duchamp's "urinal". It was a toilet sitting on a carpet of fake grass. In the vain of Duchamp they were all found objects. There was a Dracaena Marginata (dragon trees) planted in the center of the bowl of the toilet. The side of the toilet covered with color printouts of *Le Déjeuner sur l'herbe* by Eduard Manet. Art had done more than give him joy; it had found him a home.

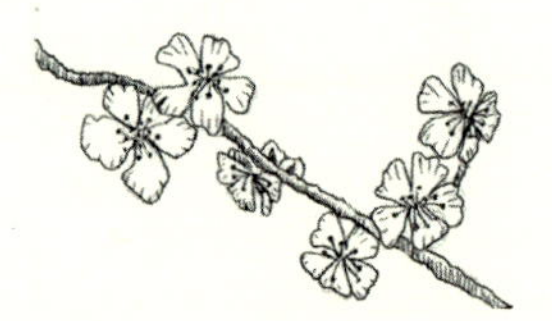

Art is Life and Life is Art

"Testing, 1-2-3- interview with James Nicolar. Check…" said the reporter checking his recording device.

"Tell me what it feels like to be part of a fashion retrospective at the MET?" the reporter asked.

"It's a great honor to be sharing the museum space with Donna Karan, Issey Miyake, and Romeo Gigli." replied James Nicolar sitting comfortably in his favorite orange chair with a plastic clear back. "I was very lucky. I was in the right place at the right time. It was a pivotal time in fashion in New York that you can still see reflected to this day."

"A lot of designers who have been through an evolution such as yours are depressed by the state of the modern fast fashion world, how do you feel about this?" the reporter asked.

James Nicolar paused and crossed his legs. The movement revealed bright orange and blue sneakers that contrasted with his immaculately pressed black pants. A slow smile crept across the handsome elder gentleman's face and his blue eyes lit up underneath dark black-framed glasses. "If I stopped being inspired why should I live? Fashion and art is living for me, not a stage of life. The idea that a designer can no longer design, make, and create fashion in NYC to compete is true. I left New York at the right time in the fashion industry early nineties. Time evolves and you have to evolve with them. An artist needs to be forward thinking. Good design and good quality control will sell no matter where you create it. Look at David Hockney, what is he in his late seventies? Not much older than me? His twelve-foot high views of Yosemite National Park completed on an IPAD, his best work yet."

After an hour, the cameraman and reporter finished up and left. James Nicolar remained seated in quiet reflection. He reached for the bottle of white wine that sat in the middle of his latest jewelry pieces on the long harvest table in his kitchen and poured a glass. He slowly sipped at the glass and enjoyed the silence. James felt content. It didn't last long. His phone was a buzzing on the table. *b there in 5,* R. It was 9 pm and soon his house would be buzzing much like the phone but it wouldn't stop. James continued to sip slowly and in a blink of an eye his doorbell rang and Ren appeared in black silk pants and one of his cardigan sweaters, a bouquet of fresh flowers, and two bags of wine bottles.

"Please help darling." Ren said kissing both cheeks of James.

"Oh, do tell me you didn't buy out the store. We are only

having a few people tonight." James said lifting a grocery bag.

"A few people James? *Wrong.* I invited more than that. I mean we *must* celebrate. This is a big deal. The MET. The caterers are parked outside, we have to make space. Now, go take a shower. I have loads to do before everyone arrives at 10 pm." Ren said as he answered the buzzer. "Out, James!" Ren shouted.

James paused and stared at the young man. Ren was the youngest of his lovers, and for a moment he felt old. Before the thought could hold, Ren shoved him in the direction of the bathroom. "Shower you, and into those new jeans I bought. At least you wore cool sneakers to the interview."

James was still laughing as he stepped into the glass door of his spa-like shower. *Water,* he thought, *doesn't it all return us to feel young and free.*

James re-entered the kitchen to the smells and sounds of sizzling garlic, onions, cilantro, and seafood lingering in the air. The caterers were busy in the kitchen and in one hour James's kitchen had been transformed into a five star restaurant. Ren had set the table with a tablecloth from Spain that was black with yellow and red embroidery that was woven from end to end. James touched the embroidery on the tablecloth that lay across his long wooden kitchen table. It was almost ritualistic for him. He loved the handmade feel and the touch and smell of the kitchen brought Spain to his apartment in Providence.

Nick arrived first along with his girlfriend Anna. James had supported Nick early on in his career. He had watched him blossom into a fine young artist. James remembered the feeling of looking through Nick's sketches and seeing the potential rawness of the young boy of fifteen. When he met Nick for the first time to speak with him, the boy was not only charming and handsome, but he had that something that all artists have; openness and hunger for more. Nick and Anna had brought two bottles of wine and flowers. James loved flowers. It wasn't just the smell of them, or the colors, it was the power they held to always draw attraction in the room. They were nature's art.

Gretchen the rock star and her new beau came next. James never thought this wild child would settle down with one man, and he was eager to learn more about her new handsome fellow. James had met Gretchen through Nick. James remembered the first time he had seen Gretchen onstage, absolutely magical and astounding—A creature not from this earth when wielding an electric guitar. James had designed a few pieces of jewelry special for her. James had chuckled when he watched an interview where Gretchen gave him a shout out about the bracelet he'd made for her and the young reporter said, "James who?" Where, Gretchen preceded (Bob Dylan style) to put the young reporter in her place for not knowing who Thee James Nicolar was. Gretchen reminded him of Debbie Harry from the band Blondie, something more than a beautiful face. She was a true artist. Gretchen brought some chocolates and two bottles of expensive Spanish Reserva.

Before long James's dining room table came to life with Spanish dishes served on a colorful array of platters, a cluster of wine bottles, and candles of varying heights that cast a beautiful glow over the nineteen people. James loved his apartment filled with people this way. Raina was the last to arrive, around the fifth course. Raina drifted in looking like Twiggy from the sixties in a checkered black and white dress, white gogo boots, and a paperboy hat. Her coat a red swing style she merely tossed over James's living room white sofa as if it belonged there. Raina's long eyelashes sparkled in shimmery mascara. Somehow when Raina entered the room it was like Audrey Hepburn in Breakfast at Tiffany's. It took your breath away. She had been James's muse for a little while. It was always a pleasure to be in Raina's company. The trick was to catch her while she stood still.

Raina came to the party with an assortment of different items she had collected that had spoken to her as "James"; A straw hat that she immediately placed on his head along with a kiss. She then placed in James's hands a framed photograph of the two of them together at a party. In the photograph, Raina was resplendent in a long paisley dress. She was draped across James's lap who held her like she was his daughter. The moment had been perfectly captured and held in time. In addition, Raina brought some Turkish figs she had been given at an event she had attended at her rich friend's house the night before. Finally, she placed a flask that she had carved James's initials in with a penknife at his table setting. Raina slid herself between Assistant Professor Henry Velazquez from Brown University and Peter Stakes a Painting Teacher from RISD. Raina always liked to be sitting with people who did not know her. James admired that adventure about Raina, but also wondered when she would make a real connection in her life. He knew what it was like to get old, and he thought the shock might be so devastating to her that she might just up and die when that time caught up with her.

"So what did I miss?" Raina asked the group as if the party was for her, and had been waiting on her to arrive.

"Oh, Raina darling, well, you missed four other amazing courses of food." James laughed, and continued, "But of course we will forgive you if you tell us what kept you away while we were enjoying the pleasure of savory of delights, good wine, and excellent conversation."

Raina began a story about meeting a famous dj at White Electric. James's eyes took in everything; an essential trait to keep a creative mind active and alive. His gaze drew him to Anna who was admiring a photograph on a side table. The photograph was of a model arms up in the air in front of a train wearing a dress by James. James moved over to stand next to Anna and enjoyed his work through fresh eyes of the young woman looking so admiringly next to him. This was a small part of pleasure an artist could momentarily rest and enjoy at a moment such as this. Lingering too long was dangerous, but at a party with good conversation and wine it was an indulgence one could revel in as an artist.

"There is something so empowering about it." Anna said. She took a sip of wine and continued to keep her eyes on the young girl in the ruffled white dress.

Anna looked at James and her cheeks flushed, "Sorry read the feminism into everything. It's also very lovely piece of clothing."

"No need to apologize Anna. She does look like she could take on the world, albeit entirely inappropriate to go to battle." James smiled warmly and took a sip of his wine. Anna smiled back. James loved this kind of intimate conversation that art could spark between people. Everyone's eyes could see the same thing so differently.

"Well, it's an exquisite dress." Anna smiled.

"Would you like to see it?" James asked.

"Really? Now." Anna said blushing.

"Well, yes, I keep my favorites on hand to remind me I must always do better. Never be satisfied. Satisfaction is death for an artist." James finished. "Come." He held out his hand to Anna.

James guided Anna down the narrow hallway to the first wooden door on the left that was bare with the exception of six metal plate letters spelling out the word STUDIO. When James opened the glass doorknob the starkness of the door did not prepare you for the overwhelming senses that awaited you inside the room. It was extremely organized but filled from the wooden floor to the high tin ceiling with color, texture, and work. Behind a simple clear modern desk one shelf contained stacked rolls of assorted fabric. Another shelf had neatly placed clear boxes that contained buttons, zippers, pencils, pins, and scissors. A third in color-coordinated order were fashion books casting a rainbow hue to the eyes; light to dark.

There were two model forms, one antique black and the other a more modern adjustable form that stood in front of the one large window in the room. On hooks against the wall where the door stood, were necklaces of varying lengths. Covering that entire wall was a photographic wallpaper scene of woods and a lake. The jewelry hung like flowers off the end of the branches on the trees in the photographic wallpaper. The soft green grass in the photograph made you feel like you could take your shoes off and walk right into the photograph and feel the grass between your toes.

On the opposite wall were a set bi-fold double doors painted bright white. James opened the closet doors and revealed to Anna a breathtaking sight of color, pattern, texture, and fabric in three rows of clothing. Below them in square cubicles were shoes in every color and style just waiting to slip onto someone's feet. Anna watched James as he walked her through snapshots of his life: a Vogue Magazine spread, New York Young Designers article, and a Rome photo shoot for a foreign film to name a few. Outfit after outfit a life story held within each carefully wrapped piece of clothing James had created with his own hands. Till he finally came to the white ruffle dress from the photograph, and slipped it out from the plastic and off the hanger. James handed the dress to Anna to hold.

"It's okay to touch Anna. It's clothing after all. It won't fall apart on you. I am an excellent seamstress too. I pride myself on excellent handicraft. I practically was born with a needle in my hands." James said with a laugh.

James watched Anna transform as she touched the chiffon fabric that moved like a light breeze. James sat down in the chair at his desk, and said, "Try it on if you like Anna. It looks like your size."

"I couldn't." Anna said looking very much like she wanted to desperately.

"Oh please do. There is nothing more indulgent for a fashion designer than a real young woman draping his hard work around her." James finished and took a sip of wine and got up to unfolded an old Japanese screen that had been leaning against the corner of the room. "You can change behind this."

Anna hesitated and then did as she was told. When she came out the dress spoke anew in the room.

"It's amazingly comfortable. I feel so different somehow. It's so lovely…I mean it makes you feel lovely. God, you wouldn't believe I am a law student at Brown. I sound like an idiot." Anna said, her cheeks flushed.

"You do look lovely in it." Nick said from the doorway. "Was wondering where you disappeared too."

Nick walked over and gave Anna a kiss and then turned to James, "I've never seen this one up close."

James smiled at the young couple then quietly slipped out of the studio. He walked back down the wooden hallway, his photographic art collection keeping him company along the way. James peaked into his living room to find the two Professors in a hot debate with Raina about the modern feminist. Ren was at the table next to Gretchen who was playing James's acoustic guitar, an Irish ballad in three quarter time. James refilled everyone's wine glass and then slid into a chair next to Gretchen's boyfriend. The wine went perfectly with the angelic sound of Gretchen's voice and the gentle strum of the strings against the wood of the guitar.

It was hard to pin who started the switch from wine to absinthe, Ren, most likely, as was his wont to always keep a party interesting. James remembered his first time drinking absinthe in the sixties. A novelist friend in New York had invited him to an absinthe party to celebrate the birthday of H.P. Lovecraft. James a fervent reader of Lovecraft brought his tales of Lovecraft's adventures on absinthe in Providence to the party. In fact, the bottle of absinthe Ren had just opened had been a gift from this same novelist. A handmade card and twine had enclosed the top of the bottle with the words "To my fellow artist, for a special occasion." James had saved the bottle as he treasured his friends' words and it had sat for years untouched on a shelf of expensive liquor bottles.

Ren read the handmade card and stated, "James, there is no bigger occasion to celebrate than the MET!"

James acquiesced and soon the ritual of preparing the absinthe began. The ritual, like the drink (also known as the green fairy) seemed to cast a certain mystical feeling in James's apartment. As if a beacon all guests were back around the kitchen table. Ren poured a glass for each guest of the green liquid that tasted like liquorice. The candles made the room warm and cozy. James watched his guests shadows grow tall in the glow of the light of the flames. Anna was still wearing the white ruffle dress and Raina had pinned her hair up with some fresh flowers from the table. James noticed Raina had draped two of his latest necklace creations around her neck. The light from the candles enhanced the geometrical shapes of the large beads and created a new pattern; a trick of the eye, or the green fairy, perhaps. James's mind always astir with creative thoughts imagined creating a necklace as complex as the revised vision he was beholding around Raina's lovely long neck.

Instinctively James caught the vision through the lens of his phone, in case the vision was merely a fantasy. Then, just as quickly he was back sipping his glass of absinthe. Gretchen's blue eyes and long lashes seem to have grown in size making her appear like a doll. Her new boyfriend's pupils were dilated so that the green of his eyes barely peeked out from behind like a solar eclipse. Together Gretchen and Liam looked like a cartoon of lovely models clad in leather garments that shone like metal. The candles in front seemed to have grown thin and pointy and the hot wax that had dripped down the sides were spreading across the wooden table like melting lava from a volcano. James touched the smooth wax feeling it slowly harden and attach itself to the surface of the wood table.

Everyone at the table seemed to be investigating the everyday items in front of them as if they were newfound treasures. James smiled at the peaceful and beautiful scene of slow life that lay before him like a lovely still life painting. Nick had begun drawing marks on Ren's hands, and he and Ren seemed as intent upon every stroke and every line. The English professor begun to recite Lovecraft's infamous poem to Edgar Allen Poe. The words hung in the air as if there was an echo in the room. Raina lay down on the white flaccati rug and began to touch the strands as if she lay in a field of green grass. The Art professor began to recount a visit to H. P. Lovecraft's gravesite in Swan Point Cemetery where his gravestone could be found. The stories, words, and the absinthe transported the listeners to the graveyard and the lilting willow trees, the feeling of the wind, the hardness of the brown earth, and the coldness of the gravestone that bore the name "Lovecraft."

Ren, either out of exhaustion or too much drink, lay his head on the table and fell asleep in the most awkward of positions. James laughed and said, "Oh Ren, my dormouse, you have had quite enough of the Mad Hatter's party. Nick helped James guide Ren to the couch and gently laid him down. He may wake yet and surprise us." James placed Raina's abandoned coat across

Ren's body and gave him a quick kiss on the forehead. Meanwhile, before James could resume his place at the table another guest needed his attention. Raina begged him to help her up and escort her to the bathroom, where she proceeded to vomit up the absinthe and what little food was in her. Having worked with models James was no stranger to this scene. Raina sat and hugged the toilet looking like a small child.

"Oh James, your necklaces." Raina said, making a limp attempt at wiping off the vomit from the adornments around her neck with the hand towel.

"Raina, now, if you had eaten more you would not be in here on the cold tile but out there on the warm rug. Off with the christened necklaces! Nothing a little bleach won't cure."

James took off the necklaces and laid them on the sink counter.

"Up my little angel. To bed." James commanded.

He tucked Raina in under the down white blanket, and with a fatherly hand gently comforted her by brushing her cheek and forehead. Raina smiled and whispered, *thanks*, as her heavy eyelids slowly closed. They opened and closed several times as if fighting the inevitable sleep that was to come. James had never been a father, and never would be, but Raina felt like a daughter. She needed caring, and a watchful older eye. Raina was wild and free, but he worried one day she might jump off a cliff and never return to this world. James sat in the dark watching over Raina like a guardian angel. Then James leaned down and kissed her cheek.

James found his other child, Ren still passed out on the livingroom couch under Raina's checkered coat. His dormouse seemed out for the night. James leaned down to kiss him again on the forehead, and a smile crept across Ren's face, but he remained asleep. James imagined he was dreaming of being a famous dancer onstage.

Upon James's return to the kitchen everyone seemed to be in full absinthe mode. The English Professor was creating art with the candles on the table. So far he had covered half of James's harvest table with concentric circles and his fingers were filled with hot wax. Gretchen had her ear pressed against the opening of the acoustic guitar, listening intently for invisible sounds. Gretchen's blue eyes illuminating what James imagined her mind was experiencing from the sensation of the wooden instrument touching her ear and the absinthe opening that portal. Gretchen's boyfriend was writing feverishly on napkins with an ink pen. The Art Professor was carefully inspecting each of the flowers that had been in the vase on the table but were now spread across the wooden floor like a science experiment. They were lined up in stages of dissection—From full bloom to merely a green stem. Nick was slowly pealing off the label of a wine bottle, and next to him five other bottles stood unsheathed, each with a disengaged label lying like discarded clothes on the floor. Anna was at the end of the table looking at an origami book and touching the pages as if she could make the creations spring to life. Everyone at his party was deep in their own mind.

James watched until the scene took on a humorous tone to him, so much so that he could not contain the laughter in him. He started laughing so loudly he thought for sure his guests would awaken from their projects of the mind and look his way, but no one except Anna did. She looked up at James with a childlike expression and said, "Do you have any origami paper?" James simply nodded his head and got up and removed a stack of origami paper from a hutch next to the dining room table. He spread out the lovely paper on the table in front of Anna. Together James and Anna inspected and discussed the quality of the design and texture for the perfect paper to begin with.

"They are so special James, are you sure we can use them?" Anna asked.

James smiled and said, "Yes. We *must.*"

"It's so hard to know which to choose? They are all such treasures—More lovely than diamonds, gold, or silver. In fact, I don't know if I have ever seen something more beautiful. Except maybe flowers, I do *so* love flowers." Anna giggled.

"Let's make some flowers." James replied. "I'll show you how."

"Oh, yes. Let's do." Anna replied her eyes wide with delight.

James spread out the square sheets of a patchwork of patterns gleaming with gold, silver, and shining like Japanese fish swimming in a pond.

"Maybe I'll just watch you do it. I wouldn't want to ruin your paper. I'm sure they aren't cheap." Anna said with her hands still caressing the embossed edges of the paper patterns with her fingertips.

"Anna your hands are still on the papers, which makes me *not* believe your words." James said laughing.

James's laugh was light and extremely contagious. Anna started laughing.

"I didn't even realize they were still there. I thought I'd let go!" Anna laughed.

Before Anna could protest more James handed her a sheet of blue and yellow flowers with silver tendrils that curled like vines around the paper.

"Do what I do, Anna." James said with a calm teacher like voice.

James folded a side and slid his hand up and down the crease in order to make the fold permanent. Anna did the same. James and Anna folded and delicately bent the will of the origami paper to slowly bloom into a round flower with petals. James loved the feel of the paper, process, and the concentration required in the process of creation. He thrived in the moment and all his senses were alert and ready. The green fairy assisted his vision to take Anna from a tight rose like pattern, to a sun like daisy, tiny chrysanthemums that were soft on the ridges, and finally an orchid. The flowers lay across the table. Anna and James admired their work.

Anna smiled at James, and James smiled at Anna. They shared a silent art moment of the adrenalin of creation to fruition. James loved this feeling of timelessness that he and Anna were in. Art could do that for anyone, anyone that would be willing to open their eyes and their mind. James picked up the first flower and gently placed it in Anna's hair. He deftly braided it into place. Anna smiled at James and looked pleased at having the art placed on her. Then without a word, James continued to place another flower in Anna's hair next to the other. Anna stood still and allowed James to create on her hair. Flower after flower soon became a crown on the top of her brown wavy hair. James took pictures and Anna obliged like a good model every direction James gave. She looked like a child getting ready to dance around the maypole in her bare feet in James's ruffle white dress, and flowers in her hair.

James then walked her over to the hallway mirror to let her look at her vision. The frame of the wooden mirror made Anna's reflection look like a framed photograph. James took one more shot of her reflection in the mirror.

"Thanks," Anna whispered.

"Let's see what Nick thinks of his girl." James said walking her back into the kitchen.

They found Nick asleep on the floor with a wine label curled around his finger like a ring. James and Anna laughed as they looked all around them and every single guest was fast asleep in mid creation. The clock on the wall told them it was five a.m. They laughed and laughed until they were both holding their stomachs in pain. James had tears streaming down his face and Anna fell on to the floor. In the process she knocked all the bottles over that Nick had stacked. This only momentarily stirred Nick and then he mumbled something unintelligible and then nothing. James helped Anna up and said, "Let's go make the best of this absinthe, to the balcony my lady."

James opened the French doors off the kitchen and Anna stepped out onto the small balcony that had just enough room for two people. The balcony was bare save two black wrought iron chairs with patterned cushions. As Anna sat down next to James she looked down at the dress.

"James, this dress is so amazing." Anna touched the fabric and traced the ruffles with her fingers.

"Thank you my darling, and now you and my dress must look up or you will miss the best experience of the party."

The sun was rising above the city of downtown Providence. They watched it move up into the sky above the balcony railing and up into the fluffy full cotton ball clouds. The colors were magnificent and glorious and the clouds reflected the light spreading its power as far as the eye could see. Anna and James sat in silence as nature created what man could only attempt to begin to imitate in art.

"The sun, it can make one feel quite ashamed of the notion of creation, or being a creator." James said, "At the same time it makes one feel like you never want to stop creating or life will not be worth living at all."

"I know what you mean." Anna said, still focused ahead at the sun that had now fully appeared in all boldness above the layer of clouds.

"James, can I ask you a question." Anna asked, "Are you afraid of death?"

James was silent.

"I'm sorry, was that a weird question? Just, I think, what if I leave this world having done nothing worthwhile? I never thought much about it. Maybe, I just began thinking about it more now that I am with Nick?" Anna finished looking like she had more to say but the words not quite formed in her brain to be spoken aloud.

"Why since you have been with Nick?" James asked gently.

"Well, ever since I can remember I have always known what I wanted to be and never questioned my direction in life. That is until now; *until* meeting Nick. This, just wasn't in my plans, yet. And it has me *so* confused." Anna replied. "Experiencing life with him has awakened a part of me I never knew existed, and well, it's not logical."

"The best parts of my life have been accidental. Things I never expected to happen." James said with a smile.

"Really?" Anna asked.

"Yes. I wasn't always comfortable with that. That's something that comes with age and experience. After awhile you just begin to trust that is a part of life to be expected. You begin to welcome it. It can be an exciting feeling; it's all in the way you look at it. Think about that sunrise we just watched. We couldn't predict how it would look or what it would become, because nature is unpredictable. We try to organize our lives, but there is a beauty in also letting go and seeing where it will go without your input too." James said.

"It seems like you artists are able to do that, like you were born that way." Anna said with a laugh. "Nick is *so* good at that. I guess it has made me begin to feel like there is something wrong with me. I over plan everything, nothing is by coincidence—Work hard, get good grades, get a job, and be successful in life. The way I have felt since I was a little child. Never doubted that direction. I had such a sense of satisfaction, but now, after… meeting Nick, I feel like…something…something has changed in me and I can't go back to feeling that way anymore. I want to travel and see the world. I want to experience life, but that wouldn't be smart or prudent." Anna finished.

"And why is that Anna?" James asked with a smile.

"Well, money for starters." Anna said. "And my career. Taking the time off before I even start? Seems unwise."

"I understand that drive, and it doesn't mean you can't do both. I was very driven like you at your age too. But if you want advice from a man who has a little life under him, allow your heart to win sometimes."

James and Anna sat silently for a while. Neither knowing time or space, nor caring. Anna awoke as if from a dream as she felt Nick's warm kiss on her cheek. She looked up to see Nick and for that moment Anna's did let her heart win. As Anna turned to look at James to thank him, she saw only an empty chair.

Acknowledgements

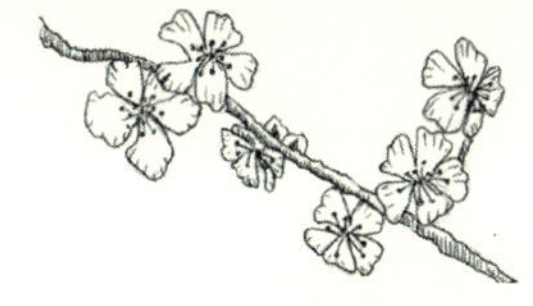

Thanks to **Bre Goldsmith**
for story collaboration and pushing me as a writer.

Thanks to **Guy Benoit** for being the first to read this book of short stories and helping me edit the book.

Thanks to my husband **Matt,**
and my daughters **Sydney** and **Elizabeth**
loves of my life.

Thanks to my parents
Nancy and Sam Raskin
best parents ever.

Thanks to **Johnna and Steve Raskin**
great sister-in-law and brother

Thanks to **Joe Propatier, Seana Carmody,**
Karen Orsi, and **Chick Graning**
for keeping music in my life.

Thanks to **everyone who bought this book**
and my other books. You ROCK!

Joyce Raskin is a writer, musician, artist, and a mom. This is her first book of short stories. Her other books are: *Aching To Be: A Girl's True Rock and Roll Story*, *The Fall and Rise of Circus Boy Blue*, and *My Misadventures as a Teenage Rock Star.* All books are available for sale on Amazon worldwide in paperback and ebook format for all devices. Joyce also plays bass guitar and sings in Scarce, Reindeer, and Speedy Consuela. Joyce also has a series of acrylic paintings on canvas.

Social media links for Joyce Raskin:
https://www.facebook.com/joycestellaraskin
https://twitter.com/scarcerocks

Reindeer Music sites:
https://www.facebook.com/pages/Reindeer/597000713650655
http://reindeer1.bandcamp.com/

Speedy Consuela Music site:
https://fortknoxfive.bandcamp.com/track/speedy-consuela-number-one-fan

Scarce Music site:
https://scarce1.bandcamp.com/

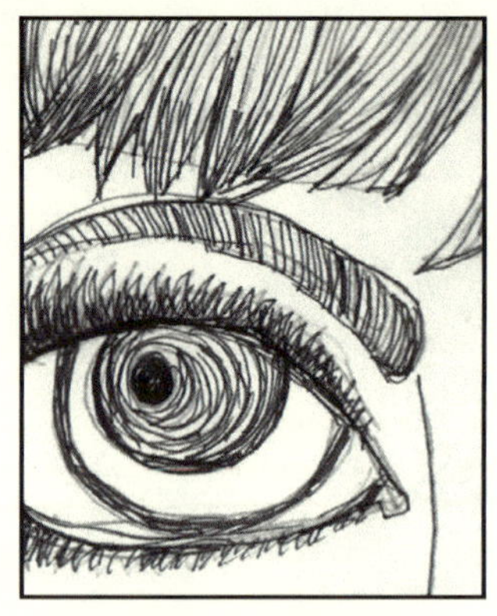

KEEP
OUT
OF YOUR
ROOM

YOUR ART
SUCKS
CRITIC
MASTER
STUDENT

HA!

POW

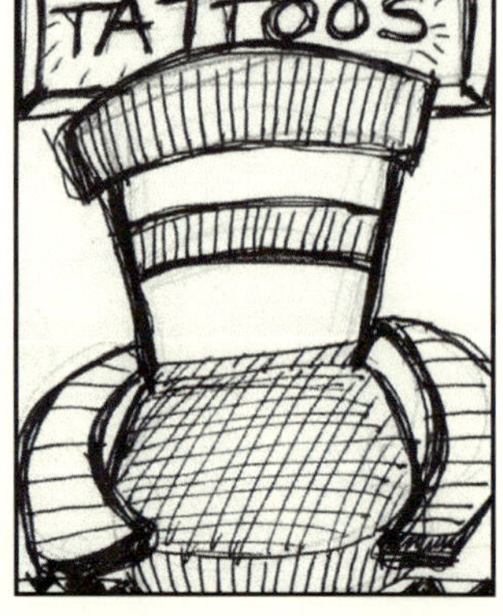
TATTOOS

MAG
ROCKER
DID YOU SEE HER
HER
WHAT A FREAK
GO
DRINK ME
STUPID PAINTER BOYS STRIKE AGAIN
JANE